continued . . .

Death Is a Cabaret

"*Death Is a Cabaret* introduces an engaging new hero in an unusual and convincing setting—the world of collectors and the extremes to which they'll go to get what they want . . . I enjoyed meeting Jeff Talbot and his unusual domestic ménage. I hope we'll see them all again soon."
—Sara Paretsky

"Deborah Morgan's witty debut is a deft blend of mystery, mayhem, and most terrifying of all, the antics of the antique world. I look forward to sleuthing and antiquing with Jeffrey Talbot again soon."   —Harlan Coben

"Lively, well-plotted . . . Deborah Morgan, an award-winning author of mystery and historical western short stories, delivers an outstanding traditional mystery in her first novel . . . Full of twists and turns . . . Collectors and antiques buffs will be thrilled with *Death Is a Cabaret*. Mystery fiction fans will find a new treasure."
—*South Florida Sun-Sentinel*

"A fascinating mystery that enables the audience to become an intricate part of the plot and will surely bring acclaim to Deborah Morgan."   —*Midwest Book Review*

"On the heels of *Antiques Roadshow*'s popularity comes an exceptional mystery series that's sure to please and tease the treasure hunter in every reader."
—*Publishers Weekly*

"A remarkable read."   —*Mystery News*

"*Death Is a Cabaret* marks the beginning of a new series that will endear itself to antique-loving mystery fans—it's more exciting than *Antiques Roadshow*!"
—*Romantic Times*

THE
MAJOLICA
MURDERS

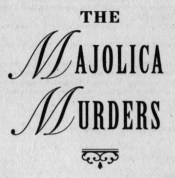

DEBORAH MORGAN

BERKLEY PRIME CRIME, NEW YORK

THE BERKLEY PUBLISHING GROUP
Published by the Penguin Group
Penguin Group (USA) Inc.
375 Hudson Street, New York, New York 10014, USA
Penguin Group (Canada), 90 Eglinton Avenue East, Suite 700, Toronto, Ontario M4P 2Y3, Canada
(a division of Pearson Penguin Canada Inc.)
Penguin Books Ltd., 80 Strand, London WC2R ORL, England
Penguin Group Ireland, 25 St. Stephen's Green, Dublin 2, Ireland (a division of Penguin Books Ltd.)
Penguin Group (Australia), 250 Camberwell Road, Camberwell, Victoria 3124, Australia
(a division of Pearson Australia Group Pty. Ltd.)
Penguin Books India Pvt. Ltd., 11 Community Centre, Panchsheel Park, New Delhi—110 017, India
Penguin Group (NZ), Cnr. Airborne and Rosedale Roads, Albany, Auckland 1310, New Zealand
(a division of Pearson New Zealand Ltd.)
Penguin Books (South Africa) (Pty.) Ltd., 24 Sturdee Avenue, Rosebank, Johannesburg 2196, South Africa

Penguin Books Ltd., Registered Offices: 80 Strand, London WC2R ORL, England

This is a work of fiction. Names, characters, places, and incidents either are the product of the author's imagination or are used fictitiously, and any resemblance to actual persons, living or dead, business establishments, events, or locales is entirely coincidental. The publisher does not have any control over and does not assume any responsibility for author or third-party websites or their content.

THE MAJOLICA MURDERS

A Berkley Prime Crime Book / published by arrangement with the author

PRINTING HISTORY
Berkley Prime Crime mass-market edition / April 2006

ISBN: 0-425-20926-1

BERKLEY® PRIME CRIME
Berkley Prime Crime Books are published by The Berkley Publishing Group,
a division of Penguin Group (USA) Inc.,
375 Hudson Street, New York, New York 10014.
The name BERKLEY PRIME CRIME and the BERKLEY PRIME CRIME design are trademarks belonging to Penguin Group (USA) Inc.

PRINTED IN THE UNITED STATES OF AMERICA

10 9 8 7 6 5 4 3 2 1

Dedication

For family:

Too many to list
Too precious to forget

Acknowledgments

I'm grateful to Dennis, Anita, Laurie, Cindy, Janet, Cathie, Zoe, and Linda—those Washington pickers and dealers who share stories and friendship with equal generosity.

Bridgette Green provided information from her career that added a layer to this story.

Rochelle Hyatt inspired the idea of opening up the conservatory with her suggestion that Sheila have an enclosed garden.

J. Michael Major suffered the inevitable typo in the acknowledgments of Jeff's last adventure. He's too much the gentleman to complain. We'll get it right this time, ink brother.

Continued support from the following core group is both welcome and essential: Dylan Brown, Loren D. Estleman, Gail Henry, Kimberly Hopper, Betty Morgan, and Kevin Williams.

Majolica (ma·jol′i·ca) (noun): Tin- or lead-glazed earthenware that is richly colored and decorated. Pieces were shipped from the Spanish port of Majorca (hence the name) to Italy in the fifteenth century, where, as products of the Italian Renaissance, they were renamed *maiolica*. Majolica was popular in England and America from about 1850 until 1900.

TRICK OR TREAT

❧

*T*HE WITCH IS missing three teeth.

She grins uncertainly, revealing the vacancies alongside two huge front teeth that she'll grow into. The hairy wart attached to her button nose, likely with spirit gum from a Halloween makeup kit, threatens to let loose. She worries it and, apparently satisfied that it's intact, holds open an orange plastic bag printed all over with cats, bats, and tombstones. "Trick or treat?" she says softly.

Shy, Jeff Talbot thinks as he studies her; dressed all in black with a witch's hat nearly as tall as she is. He tries to remember what grade he was in when baby teeth gave way to permanent ones, but it's been too long.

"Treat, for being the prettiest witch in Seattle." He hopes he can help her relax a little, enjoy the holiday. It's one thing to be afraid in front of your class at school, another thing altogether to carry your insecurities into every facet of your childhood. She looks familiar, something about her large, sad eyes. But he realizes that it's the shyness that gives her the wide-eyed, anticipatory gaze.

With each costumed child, Jeff searches for one telling characteristic—something that isn't part of a packaged costume. The boy who preceded the witch in line sported a black right eye. He wore red satin prizefighter shorts and matching red boxing gloves. He didn't need the makeup kit.

"Did that shiner inspire your costume," Jeff asked him, "or did you get in the ring with another guy *because* of the costume?"

"I got the black eye playing football," the boy said, "so Dad"—he jerked his head toward the man standing behind him—"came up with the idea."

The man, dressed in a white shirt and black trousers, had a towel draped around his neck, probably replacing the necktie from his day at some downtown office. He slapped the kid on the back a couple of times. "It'll make him tough."

Jeff winced slightly, as acutely aware as the boy that the father has a heavy hand. Jeff's own childhood was a series of those backslaps—both physical and psychological—from the stern grandfather who raised him. He hoped the kid who stood in front of him would grow fast and strong, and put to good use a sports scholarship to college.

Jeff threw an extra handful of treats into the prizefighter's sack.

He focuses on the witch poised before him, waits for her to ascend the stairs. It's a banner year for little ghosts and goblins, and kids dressed as their favorite superheroes and hip-hop stars. Jeff reaches into the large stainless-steel bowl full of candy that his butler, Greer, found to replace the huge yet now-empty plastic jack-o'-lantern, and withdraws a large clump of individually wrapped bubble gum, jawbreakers, and miniature candy bars. While he's doing this, he wonders again about the girl's missing teeth and whether her parents consider the effect that the sugar will have on the remaining molars and bicuspids. (Her father, standing two stair steps below his daughter, is dressed like Darth Vader, right down to the mask and boots, and sporting a lightsaber that looks more like a mop handle in a nylon sheath.)

"Go on," Darth Vader growls as he nudges the girl-witch.

Jeff's chest tightens. *Impatience will be the downfall of America.*

The witch advances to the next step.

For years after that fateful night, Jeff Talbot would ponder the details, waffling between his own shortcomings (*I should've been studying the characteristics of the* adults, *not the* kids) and the use and abuse of children in this screwed-up world.

There would be no memory blackout, and he would recall every movement as if he'd been outside himself, watching it play out on the front porch of someone else's home.

He reaches toward the witch's bag, holding the fistful of sweets in one hand and cradling the bowl against his torso with the other, when two things happen simultaneously: Poe, released from his birdcage on the porch by a kid who sneaks up and swings open the door, flies screeching and flailing toward Jeff as Darth Vader scoops up the girl-witch with his left arm and points the lightsaber in his right hand at Jeff's chest.

Instinctively, Jeff lifts the bowl as he twists to avoid the panicked crow. Too late he sees a flash, followed by a puff of smoke, then a spurt of flames licking the tip of the cheap nylon sheath. *Not a lightsaber, not a saber at all. A gun.* The bullet cuts through the stainless-steel bowl with a resonating *ping* and strikes him in the chest.

The large bowl flips into the air and showers the steps with bright candies as the villain and his little witch flee. Two boys dressed in Spider-Man costumes waiting behind the pair in black, squeal and hit the floor, snatching up the goodies.

Jeff struggles against the catapulting force, watches the stainless-steel bowl strike the porch boards—*gong*—then clang and warp its way toward the pair of superheroes. Startled, they run screaming down the steep stairs, followed by a string of frightened children. It puts Jeff in mind of ribbons on a kite's tail, and the kite disappears as he falls backward and for one light-headed second he thinks he's watching it fall from the sky.

He lands deadweight across the threshold. He tries to blink, but his eyelids won't respond. Staring, he first sees Greer's face, then the face of his wife, Sheila. *An angel.* He starts to speak, but he can't breathe, he can't breathe. . . .

ONE

~~~~~~

$\mathcal{S}$HEILA SUCKED IN air. "What are you *doing* here?"

Jeff Talbot finished jotting "Oct 11" in its appropriate space on the blank check. He'd hoped his wife wouldn't walk past the library he also used as his home office. He looked up from the checkbook. "I live here, remember?"

"But you're not supposed to be back till six. And, even then, you're under strict orders to go straight up the front stairs and get ready. I've got all sorts of . . . things going on for your birthday party tonight, and I don't want it spoiled."

Jeff looked up at his wife and faked a blank look. "Today's my birthday?"

"Jeff Talbot, don't toy with me."

Sheila had been working on the plans for his official Over-the-Hill Birthday Dinner for months, planning a gourmet meal for a small group of friends, ordering decorations for the all-black theme to commemorate Jeff's Big

Four-Oh, even hinting that she'd ordered a formal black gown to wear. More important, though, she'd given him strict rules for the day, and he'd broken Rule Number One: Don't.

He grinned. "Sorry, hon. Forgot my checkbook."

As Jeff finished speaking, Lanny leaned around the wing of the large Queen Anne chair that faced Jeff's desk, and gave Sheila a timid wave.

She started slightly. "Oh. Hi, Lanny. I didn't know you were here."

"Sorry, Mrs. Talbot. I thought you could see me." Lanny—who might just as well have been named Lanky—was, like Jeff, an antiques picker. The similarities stopped there. While Jeff still looked like an FBI agent much of the time (despite his attempts to dress down and lighten up), Lanny looked like someone who slept in a refrigerator box and warmed his hands over fires banked in rusty barrels. His long brown ponytail splayed out from under a well-worn black knit sock cap, and his scruffy beard helped to offset his thinness and leave one guessing at his age. He wore tightly woven gloves with the fingers cut out, and a pea coat—vintage forties. His vacant gaze seemed to dissipate only a little when he addressed Sheila, and Jeff realized that he'd rarely seen it completely lift.

Jeff smiled at his wife. "Lanny found something I've been interested in for awhile. His contact's holding it till the end of the day. So you see, I had no choice."

Sheila gave him a look, which said everything, then turned her attention to Lanny. "I wish you'd reconsider tonight's party."

Lanny looked down. "Thanks, but I'm not into crowds."

It was Jeff's turn. He gave Sheila a look, warning her not to push it.

She said, "Well, come on by if you change your mind. Blanche and Trudy will be here."

"Yes, ma'am. Thank you."

Somewhere along the way, Lanny had learned manners. Jeff had witnessed this for years. But as for a social life, Jeff suspected that he didn't have much of one. Even as Jeff thought this, he realized that he was stereotyping. Of course, everything he thought about Lanny's appearance would be construed as stereotyping by most. Jeff would argue, though, that he truly saw the advantage of the look, having done a little undercover work during his years with the Bureau. Likely, many stood in judgment of the man, but Jeff considered his appearance useful. With the look, Lanny could pass for any number of people: a fisherman down at the piers that embroidered Puget Sound, an outpatient of a ward for the terminally ill, one of the city's growing number of homeless. Still, Jeff had to admit he wouldn't be surprised to learn that Lanny had celebrated his latest birthday with a package of Twinkies and a can of Coke in the shadows beside a convenience store.

Jeff didn't know the man's birthday, let alone his age, but he guessed him to be in his early thirties. He also didn't know the young man's last name or, actually, much at all about him. The one thing he knew for sure, the only thing he'd ever needed to know, was that he could trust the guy completely.

Lanny had been one of Jeff's informants back when he was an agent. Jeff had marveled at Lanny's streetwise nature and wondered whether the man had been on the streets most of his life. He seemed to know how to disappear into the shadows, blend into the woodwork, hide in a space no larger than a shoebox.

Jeff knew that Lanny wouldn't show for the party, and he knew that Sheila knew it, too.

"Oh!" Sheila said. "Did Jeff show you the conservatory?"

"He did. It's astounding—the architecture, the size, the stained glass. I couldn't believe it was there. I mean, from the outside you can't even tell."

Jeff thought, *He doesn't know how much it helps that he said that.*

"Did Jeff put you up to saying that?"

"No, ma'am." Lanny looked bewildered. "I—it's just—well, it's huge when you're standing in it, but, well, like I said, it's totally hidden from the street."

Sheila shot Jeff a look. He raised his hands in defense. "I didn't say a word, Sheila, I swear."

She arched a brow, accompanied by an expression that belied complete relief, then sat kitty-cornered from Lanny and clasped her hands at her knees. "It's great, isn't it? I just have a few more things to do to it, a few more pieces I want to add."

Opening the Victorian home's conservatory had come about by circumstance. Sheila, an accomplished chef, had become so irritated when she couldn't lay hands on a particular fresh herb for a new dish she wanted to try, that she had blurted out, "I wish there were some way I could grow my own!" Seattle's climate didn't offer much hope for indoor plants that required a fair amount of sun, and, although Sheila was gaining ground in her struggle with agoraphobia, she hadn't yet advanced to the stage of leaving her home.

Quite by accident, Greer had found a solution. While reviewing old ledgers on the home itself, in order to check early records of maintenance, the butler had located the original architectural plans and had suggested opening up the old conservatory.

Jeff had forgotten all about that segment of the Queen Anne home. The glass walls were obscured on the outside by walls of ivy, evergreens, and hearty antique roses that had somehow survived Jeff's bachelor years without attention. The French doors leading from the drawing room to the anteroom and subsequent beveled- and stained-glass conservatory had been totally concealed by a massive rococo armoire pressed into service as a coat closet.

Jeff glanced from Lanny to Sheila and back. Fortunately, Lanny gave no indication that he was in on acquiring one of the special pieces Sheila wanted for her new decorating project. Even if he had, though, she was clearly too excited to notice.

"What do you think of my feathered friends?" Sheila asked.

Lanny said, "They're cool. Did you have them before?"

"No, but they seemed like a logical addition. The crow is named Edgar Allan Poe—Poe for short—the African Grey is Bargain Basement, and the Amazon parrot—that's the multi-colored one—is Morty."

Jeff made no secret of how he felt about the birds. "The squawking at night is keeping me awake. I feel like I'm living in the boarding house in *The Ladykillers*—the original, not the remake. You ever see that one?"

Lanny nodded. "That's why you drape their cages in the evening, to tell them it's bedtime."

Sheila grinned sheepishly. "I know I'm supposed to, but that seems cruel, somehow."

"Look at it this way," Lanny said. "They need their sleep, just like you do. You'd be doing them a favor."

"I hadn't thought about it like that. Thanks." She turned to Jeff. "Patience, okay? While I give that a try?"

"Sure, as long as you don't get a bird large enough to fit the Jurassic Park terrarium." That was Jeff's nickname for the long-empty Wardian case they'd found in the center of the conservatory's floor.

Sheila responded, "That's for plants, and I almost have enough now to fill it."

When they'd first gained access to the conservatory, they found that it contained several Victorian birdcages in various sizes, and an assortment of rusty cast-iron urns, fountains, and garden furniture. Along the edges of the large, octagonal room with its domed ceiling topping out at two stories high, was a jumble of stacked jardinieres, and when Sheila first discovered them, she set about ordering aspidistras (because they could survive with very little light), along with ferns, fuschia, heliotrope, fragrant orange trees, white jasmine, poppies, and Jeff wasn't sure what else.

"My culinary studies included plants and flowers," Sheila said. "You don't want the perfumes of your center-pieces to overwhelm the aromas and tastes of the meals you've prepared."

"And," Jeff said, "you don't want to poison your guests by mistaking edible flowers for inedible ones in your recipes."

Doctor Jen had been right, convincing Sheila that the light would help lift her spirits by increasing her seratonin levels—hard enough to obtain during fall and winter in Seattle. The conservatory, which was on the west side of the home (clearly to take advantage of any afternoon light), was separated from the drawing room by an anteroom. Nothing more than a glass-walled corridor, it posed one of the biggest challenges for Sheila. But Greer had arranged for gardeners to come in and strategically sculpt the vintage plants that had overtaken the exterior, making sure to leave plenty of foliage so that Sheila didn't feel exposed.

It had taken a solid week for five of them (Jeff and Sheila, along with Greer and their twice-a-week house-keepers—spinster sisters Lucy and Polly Wing) to scrub down its interior, rid it of the dank smell, and make the glass sparkle.

That's when Sheila discovered the Wing sisters' talents as designers and seamstresses. She hired them to cover cushions for the wicker and bamboo furniture in barkcloth depicting palm fronds and tropical colors.

Sheila said, "The Wing sisters helped me decorate. Do you know them, Lanny?"

"No, ma'am."

"They're the ones who suggested acquiring the birds from Liem's Pet Shop in the International District—as long as I didn't get one named Polly."

"It's a good place," Lanny said.

Jeff sensed that Lanny had reached his saturation point

for socializing. He said, "We'd better go, if you're going to close that deal today."

Sheila stood, and Lanny followed suit. "Good luck with . . . everything," he said.

"Thanks. I'm afraid I tend to get carried away. I hope I didn't keep you too long."

"Not at all." He bowed slightly.

Jeff looked at Sheila. "I'm giving Lanny a lift back downtown."

"Just make sure you leave through the front door. I've got your party decorations all over the kitchen and dining room." She pointed a warning finger at him, told Lanny good-bye, then disappeared down the corridor.

When she was gone, Lanny said, "She seems okay now."

"Yeah." Jeff let out a deep sigh. "It was rough going after she was kidnapped, and I was afraid her agoraphobia would get the better of her for the rest of her life. But she's gained a lot of ground since then, found a doctor who's done wonders—obviously, or she'd never have been able to tackle the conservatory. It's been a big step for her."

"Hard to believe that was two years ago. The kidnapping."

"Yeah, but thanks to you, we got to her before . . . Well, I don't want to think about what would've happened if you hadn't helped find her."

"Don't go advertising it. I like to stay under the radar."

This Jeff knew, and had never pried. But a window had been opened a couple of inches, so he reached inside. "Any particular reason?"

Lanny scratched his neck. "Keep people guessing, I suppose. I've always liked my privacy. Now, with all the trouble over identity theft and credit-card scams, I'm glad I've kept things close to the vest."

"It's getting harder to do, though, isn't it?"

"Nah. I've got my systems and sources. And, a mattress stuffed with cash, of course." Jeff caught the slight, and rare, glint in Lanny's eye when he smiled noncommittally, but Jeff couldn't read whether or not the guy was telling the truth. No matter. Lanny could have a mattress stuffed with nothing *but* cash, and Jeff wouldn't care. The picker/informant had always played fair, always been reliable, and Jeff owed him his life. He *had* been instrumental in finding Sheila after her kidnapping, and had provided valuable information about Seattle's underbelly several times over.

Jeff said, "Are you sure a check won't be a problem? We can swing past my bank, get cash instead." Although the two men had worked this sort of deal many times before, the amount had been smaller and Jeff had always given Lanny cash.

"I don't live *that* far under the radar." Lanny waggled a finger at the checkbook. "Make it out to John Smith."

John Smith? Why hadn't Lanny mentioned that before? Perhaps, because it sounded so . . . *alias?*

"What?" Lanny said innocently, in response to Jeff's raised brow. "I've even got an ID that says so."

Jeff thought he detected Lanny's mouth twitch slightly but he did as asked and scribbled "John Smith" on the pay-to-order-of line. He didn't care if the guy's ID read "Lanny Shmanny." He wasn't going to quibble.

Jeff ripped out the check and led the way out of the house.

After they'd gotten on the road, Jeff said, "Where to from here?"

"Just head toward Pioneer Square." Lanny brushed his fingers along the wood-paneled door. "You sure keep this car in good shape."

Jeff started to bemoan the bucks he'd poured into the '48 Chevy woodie but guilt stopped him. Last he knew, Lanny's ride was held together with wire and wishes. He said, "She's built tough, I suppose."

Lanny nodded.

"Still got your pickup?" Jeff said.

"Sure, but she needs a lot of work. I'll be able to get

new tires, stuff like that, after today." He stole a glance at Jeff, then added, "Thanks."

"What for? You're doing me a big favor."

"Yeah, but you could've just as easily found this set."

"Not true. I've been working a lot over around Spokane, Moses Lake, that area. I'm usually gone three or four days at a time. Good majolica's not that easy to find." Jeff didn't tell Lanny—and hoped he didn't suspect—that he left the local trade for the young picker, assuming that it was more of a challenge for him to finance the farther jaunts.

"Having much luck?"

"Oh, some. I don't like the early mornings at the estate sales, though." Jeff drove down Second Avenue, watched the stale green light at the corner, and anticipated its change to yellow by letting up on the accelerator. A couple of girls, chatting as they walked, stepped into the street without looking.

Jeff squashed the brakes. The woodie's tires squealed, echoed by the girls, who froze.

The light turned yellow, then red, and the tide of pedestrians carried the stunned pair across the intersection.

"Here's good." Lanny extended his hand. "Thanks, man."

Jeff shook it. The fingerless glove's palm was well-worn, the fabric pilled and nubby.

Lanny opened the door and crawled from the car as he said, "I'll call you when I've got it." He didn't look back.

Jeff watched Lanny brace himself against the raw wind that blew from the Sound and glued baggy, threadbare carpenter jeans against his stick legs. Lanny drew his shoulders up around his ears and disappeared around a corner. Jeff hoped the profit Lanny would make from this deal might do more for the young man than simply buy tires. Much more.

TWO
※

*E*ERIE NOTES FROM a dirge reached the second floor as Jeff checked his appearance in the full-length mirror. *I don't* feel *forty,* he thought as he studied his features, unsure when the crow's feet had walked into the corners of his eyes, and when the taut skin along his chiseled jawline had started going slack. Up until now, he'd been too busy to think about it, too caught up in work to notice. Meanwhile, where had the time gone?

Sheila had told him that the lines were sexy, made him look mischievous when he grinned, and had assured him that his strong jawline was still very much intact. Still, he wondered if man went from forty to eighty in a downhill flight that took place over the course of eight hours' sleep. He felt as if he were standing at the top of a mountain, and that the next step would put him teetering on some pinnacle. He was sure he'd go from disbelief to death in a single step over the crest.

Sheila had acted as if she'd waited years for his fortieth so that she could play with the over-the-hill theme. Fortunately for her, his birthday was near enough to Halloween that she could easily find items to create an evening of playful lament over the passing of her husband's youth: widow's weeds for herself, Dracula's dark cape to drape over his tux (she'd announced it would be a formal, but fun, evening). Three weeks later, they would add harvest orange — pumpkins, Indian corn, turned leaves — to all the blackness for the trick-or-treaters.

The doorbell chimed, snapping him back to reality. He checked his watch — six-fifty — and started toward the bedroom door. Then he remembered Sheila's warning: He was not so much as to peek outside their room until she came to get him.

He paced, listened, heard the occasional faint voice rise from the foyer, but couldn't make out who any of the voices belonged to. He didn't know whether or not Sheila's ploy had been to build anticipation but, if so, it had worked: When at last she showed up to get him, he was as excited as a six-year-old on his way to Chuck E. Cheese's.

Sheila was dressed like Morticia except, thank God, she hadn't gone as far as covering her honey-blonde hair with a black wig.

Although she wouldn't share the guest list with him, she had assured him that it would be just a few close friends. Now, he was anxious to discover who had ventured out to help him step over the threshold and into Middle Age.

Sheila directed him to the drawing room. As they entered, Greer reached for the light switch. Jeff stopped him. He suspected that the butler was about to announce him by flashing the lights on and off, as if they were in the theater (and, considering the way the guests were dressed, they might as well have been).

Jeff took in the scene. Rarely was the drawing room decorated with such extravagance. Shimmering black and silver streamers tethered helium-filled balloons to large bouquets of eggplant-black roses. Groups of sterling candlesticks gripped glowing black tapers, and thin bands of fog curled into nothingness from somewhere behind the vases. Jeff suspected dry ice.

Sheila had achieved humor without sacrificing taste. The black balloons were printed with white tombstones sporting such epitaphs as "Four Oh My!" "R.I.P. Talbot Youth," and the ubiquitous "Lordy, Lordy, Jeffrey's Forty."

Engaged in conversation in the middle of the room were Blanche Appleby, owner of All Things Old, Seattle's largest antiques mall; her Girl Friday, Trudy Blessing; and Sam Carver and his wife, Helen. Sam and Jeff were childhood friends.

Blanche was in her seventies, but you couldn't tell it. Her effervescence, combined with coppery red hair, made her seem larger than life (in real life, she was under five feet tall). Her assistant, Trudy, could easily have been Encyclopedia Brown's big sister. She had brown hair, large round eyeglasses, and an innate curiosity about things. Both women wore vintage gowns, all in black with sequins and jets that winked in the light. Blanche, the flamboyant one, wore feathered and glittered combs in her hair.

Neither Sam nor Helen Carver had shown any signs of aging over the last fifteen years. Their deep brown skin warmed with each passing year, as if Sam had found a magical way to use the mahogany pigments he employed to restore antique furniture as a human preservative. Helen wore a black toga and headdress woven with purple and gold metallic threads. Her profile put Jeff in mind of Nefertiti. Sam tugged several times at the bow tie and cummerbund, clearly chosen to match his wife's threads.

The four turned, as if they sensed Jeff's presence. When they saw the guest of honor, they applauded. Jeff played along, sweeping the cape in an elaborate arc as he bowed.

They surrounded him then, exchanging hugs and slaps on the back, offering congratulations and condolences with equal amusement.

"Now, birthday boy," said Sheila, "I have a surprise. *Two,* actually." She called out, "It's time," and a pair stepped like a vision from the fog that enveloped the entrance to the conservatory: Gordy Easthope, Jeff's former FBI partner and dear friend; and Sheila's sister, Karen Gray.

Jeff's jaw dropped. He said to Sheila, "How'd you manage this one?" Without waiting for an answer, he tramped across the room and embraced them both.

When he looked back, Sheila was practically dancing. And that was all the birthday present he needed.

Greer approached with a tray of black-stemmed crystal, and Jeff took a flute of golden bubbly. The crowd collectively lifted its glasses and sang out, "Cheers!" He bowed again, slightly this time, and drank.

After a moment of everyone talking and laughing, conversations became more one-on-one.

Gordy buttonholed Jeff. "If the FBI gets wind of your old age, they'll put me out to pasture like a broken-down nag. I've got more years on you than I care to think about."

Jeff took a canapé from a silver tray that Greer offered. The diamond-shaped foundation was slathered with a snow-white concoction, and topped with Beluga caviar, clearly chosen for the black theme. "You're ageless, Gordy, don't you know that?"

"Yeah, yeah," the bear of a man said. "Tell it to my lumbago."

"Your being here surprises me more than anyone— even Karen. Who's minding the Windy City?"

"Your wife could persuade an arms dealer to throw his weapons off the West Seattle Bridge. She made me promise to be here for your fortieth back when you turned thirty-nine."

Jeff's brows raised. Before he could respond, though,

Sam Carver walked up, bear-hugged his friend of three dozen years. "Forty years old," he said with a tone of disbelief.

"Yeah," Jeff said, "but you'll look forty till you're at least sixty. What is it with you black guys?"

"I don't know about the looks," Sam said, "but we feel it. Thing is, we're just too cool to show it." He feigned a right jab. "This is cool, though. Better than the April Fool's theme mine is."

It *was* cool. Sheila had outdone herself.

"Helen looks better than ever," Gordy said. "Who'd believe she has five grown daughters?"

"Don't you know how that works? She looks so good on account of all the TLC I've given her over the years."

Gordy cleared his throat. "I knew I should've worn boots."

Jeff laughed, enjoying the camaraderie and comedy that the three men rarely had opportunity to share outside their annual fishing trips.

They drifted toward the conservatory, where a full-blown fog machine was at work, and the birds' cages were draped with sheer black organza. It made the birds look as if they'd been smudged with coal.

Trudy spoke to Bargain Basement, who was nervously quick-stepping along his wooden-dowel perch in a cage shaped like the Taj Mahal. Jeff approached them. "Trudy, you still collect birdcages, don't you?"

"Yes, but nothing like these. I don't have the space. Sheila was generous enough, though, to give me a small one that she found in here while cleaning up."

Sheila announced dinner, then led the group toward the dining room. As they walked, Karen looped her arm through Jeff's. He said, "You're looking lovely, Miss Gray. I hardly recognized you without the punked-up hair." The chestnut locks were secured at the nape of her neck with a black sequined clasp.

"The Southwest has mellowed me. A little."

"Sheila's shown me some of your photo credits. I'm impressed."

"Thanks. I love being my own boss." One never knew what part of the world Karen might be in, now that she'd left *National Geographic* and was freelancing. Her photo credit might be spotted in Paris's *Expatica* as easily as in the *Tucson Weekly* or the *Washington Post*.

The dining room table was dressed all in black and silver, and Jeff studied the menu card—black calligraphy on silver stock—while the others found their places. It read:

Smoked Salmon Tarts
Romaine, Orange, and Kiwi with Poppy Seed Dressing
Stuffed Pork Chops with Currant Glaze
Black Ravioli with Pumpkin Cream Sauce
Harvest Vegetables
Bird's Nest Potatoes
Dinner Rolls
Italian Cream Cake with Vanilla Bean Ice Cream

"I'd better pace myself," Jeff said as Greer set the first course in front of him.

Greer circled the table, and had just finished distributing the plates when the phone rang.

"Who on earth could that be?" Sheila said. "Everyone we know is in this room."

Jeff smiled. That was likely how Sheila felt, although any number of people might be calling.

"I'll see to it, Mrs. Talbot," Greer said.

The butler returned almost immediately, and said to Jeff, "Sir, it's Mister . . . it's Lanny, sir."

Lanny? Jeff scooted back his chair. "He knows about tonight's dinner. I wonder why he didn't wait to call?" As he stood, Greer said, "Actually, sir, he says he must speak with Mrs. Appleby."

Jeff stopped, looked at Blanche. Her mouth opened and closed a couple of times like a fish, then she recovered, excused herself, and followed Greer out of the room.

Jeff sat back down. His mind crowded with questions: Why would Lanny call Blanche? Had he noticed something at her antiques shop? A fire? Or a break-in? Maybe he'd seen the cops down there investigating something, and wanted to give Blanche a heads-up. Was he able to acquire more majolica than he'd originally thought, and was dealing with Blanche, too? Was the picker so desperate that he'd interrupt dinner, knowing Jeff's birthday celebration was underway?

"Karen," Helen Carver said, filling the silence, "where are you off to after this?"

"Great stuff going on! I'm doing a celebrity shoot at the Empress Hotel on Vancouver, then hitting a few spots across Canada before making my way down to Key West. Then it's New Orleans, San Antonio, and back to Arizona, where I just came from. I'm going to winter down there."

"Who's the celebrity?"

"They won't tell me, which means it's either a current major player, or a legend."

Sheila said, "I'm surprised you took the assignment. You usually don't play those games."

"With what the magazine's paying me, I don't care if I have to shoot Mr. Ed."

"Sign of a real pro," said Sam.

Blanche returned and dropped onto her chair. She stared at her plate for several seconds. She seemed pale but Jeff thought it might be from all the black she was wearing.

"That was quick," Jeff said. "Everything okay?" He immediately felt foolish. Anyone could see that the woman was not okay.

"Hardly. Lanny's been arrested for murder."

THREE

❦

"*M*URDER?" JEFF SAID. "You have to be joking."

"It's no joke, Jeffrey." Blanche sipped water from the goblet Trudy handed to her. "Apparently, he's been at the precinct since late this afternoon. The only reason he called was so someone would know his whereabouts."

"Well," Jeff said, standing, "you're not going down there alone, Blanche. I'll drive you. Sheila, I'm sorry, but—"

"No, I totally agree. In fact, I see no other way around it."

"Jeffrey," Blanche said. "He doesn't want anyone to come. I insisted, but he was adamant. He hung up the phone without even saying good-bye."

"That's unusual," Jeff said.

"Highly unusual." Blanche frowned.

"Something else?" Jeff asked.

"He was edgy, almost caustic. He said, 'I won't be making that delivery to you tomorrow. And tell Jeff the item I was getting for him was gone when I went back to the store—along with the shop owner.' "

"Why would he tell you that?"

"Because the shop owner was the murder victim."

A candle's flame flickered. Jeff sat back down. Lanny wouldn't kill a dealer simply for not holding on to the majolica. Lanny wouldn't kill anyone, period. "Did he tell you who it was?"

"Not at first. Then I reminded him that several of the other shop owners are my friends. This one wasn't, though."

Jeff knew that Blanche could get along with just about anybody. And, with the knowledge that this was the exception, he quickly had a name. "Fiona Brock."

"Fiona Brock." Blanche nodded. "That old bat. I could give the police a whole *list* of people who've threatened to kill Fiona at one time or another—not to her face, usually, but you know what I mean."

Jeff smiled in spite of the situation. "That old bat," as Blanche had called her, was probably younger than her red-headed competition. She looked older, though. Jeff hadn't seen Fiona Brock in three or four years. At that time, she'd had white hair worn in a contemporary-looking pageboy with bangs that were a few months past due for a trim. She kept pushing the bangs out of her eyes, and the sides were tethered above her ears with jawlike clips. She wore half-glasses for reading but they were too large for her face and she always kept her head down in order to see over them.

"What I'd like to know," Blanche was saying, "is why they threw Lanny in jail for it?"

Jeff said, "Although Fiona couldn't seem to get along with the other antiques proprietors around Seattle, I've always heard that she was relatively fair with her pickers."

Gordy said, "Well, since Lanny wouldn't tell you anything, you can figure on one of three scenarios: Number one, he got caught with his hand in the cookie jar. Or, in this case, the weapon in his hand. Number two, somebody either saw him in the act, or leaving the scene, or arguing with the woman—something like that." Gordy paused, rubbed his bottom lip with his thumb. Jeff had seen this many times, and he braced himself for what was coming next.

Blanche prompted, "Well? What's number three?"

Gordy looked up. "Confession."

Everyone talked at once.

Helen said, "Could he have done it?"

Karen said, "You were buying something from Lanny who was buying it from an antiques shop? Why didn't you just buy it yourself?"

Waving her off, Sheila said, "It's a locator thing."

Sam said, "You know, Jeff, maybe you should go down to police headquarters anyway."

Trudy said, "I agree."

Blanche said, "Me, too, I suppose, although I know Lanny well enough to know that it probably won't do any good. On the other hand, I hate to think of him in there when I'm sure he didn't kill anybody."

"Okay, okay." Jeff scissored his arms in front of him like a football ref signaling "dead ball." He had already considered all of this. He wanted to help. Lanny was more than a fellow picker, and more than the most trustworthy informant Jeff had ever had during his years as an agent. He had been instrumental in saving Sheila's life. "Blanche is right. Lanny wouldn't kill anyone."

Yes, Jeff wanted to help. But he didn't know that he could, if Lanny didn't want help. But Jeff could at least try to find out what had happened.

"Jeff," Sheila said, "we have to help him."

He looked at her, knew from her expression that she, too, was remembering his loyalty. And, she didn't even know Jeff's history with Lanny as an informant, although Jeff suspected she had assumed as much somewhere along the way. She'd always been astute that way, knowing to trust Jeff when it came to people, knowing that he'd had connections, a life, before her, knowing that, for everyone's safety, there were things he'd never share.

Jeff shrugged. "I can try, but you know Lanny. It might take something more earth-shattering than an arrest for murder to get him to open up."

Jeff's thoughts drifted. He didn't know what was in Lanny's past that had caused the man to be so secretive. He'd merely accepted it, seen it as an advantage while Lanny had been his informant. By all appearances, Lanny existed simply, wasn't into material wealth, survived meagerly on the money earned by feeding the material obsessions of others. Jeff prided himself in remembering who collected what—sometimes before he could even remember the collector's name. He'd cross-referenced his computer files to accommodate this. If he entered "Arts and Crafts furniture," he got a list of four collectors; "Shelley china"—only one, because Mrs. Shelley bought every piece of the delicate stuff that Lanny could lay his hands on (and, in turn, informed the club that her genie had unearthed another treasure for her); barbershop memorabilia: two collectors; typewriters: three. Jeff didn't know if Lanny's approach was similar but he'd always assumed that Lanny didn't own a computer. Until this moment, though, Jeff realized that he knew almost nothing about the man. Lanny might have old cream cans full of gold coins buried somewhere, for all he knew. Maybe he was one of those guys who stacked newspapers in his apartment till they avalanched, burying him and all his money. . . .

"Jeff?" Sheila touched his arm. "Are you okay?"

He looked around. Everyone at the table was staring at him. He dragged himself back to the present. "Sorry. I was just trying to remember—"

"Well," Karen said as she attacked a piece of home-made bread with her butter knife, "in the time you've been sitting here gazing off into space, you could've bailed him out already."

"Karen," Sheila said, her tone heavy with warning, "Jeff knows what he's doing."

After giving his wife a clandestine look that said *no I don't,* he spoke. "If Lanny's refusing to talk—which is highly likely—then there won't be much change over the next couple of hours. Remember, too, it's Saturday night. He probably won't get an arraignment till Monday morning. In the meantime, I can try to persuade him to accept help but it'll be a challenge, if not an impossibility. Why don't we go ahead and enjoy this fabulous dinner that Sheila's prepared, and I'll go down to the precinct when we're through, see if he'll talk to me after he's had time to think."

Trudy said, "Maybe Mr. Easthope could go with you."

Gordy drank some wine. "I'm afraid not. I'd have to announce my vocation, which would blow the minds of the Seattle cops, make it appear that Lanny's being looked at on a federal level, and probably make the guy clam up even more. Since Jeff's no longer an agent, he'll be a lot more help than I'd be."

"Gordy's right," Jeff said. "His involvement could put this whole mess on a very different level."

Helen said, "Are you sure he couldn't have killed someone?"

"Well, I am," said Sheila.

"I agree," said Blanche.

"Me, too," said Trudy.

Sam said, "Sounds like the guy has a chick fan club."

Jeff, who'd been studying Sheila's face, turned to Sam. "I'm in it, too, then. He didn't do it."

"I'd like to agree with all of you," Gordy said. "But do we ever really know what another human being is capable of, given the right circumstances?"

"When you put it that way," Karen said, "I suppose all of us are *potentially* able to take a life."

Jeff glanced at Sheila before picking up his glass of wine.

She took the signal, asked Greer to serve the next course.

The news definitely changed the tone of the party, and the black decorations were truly fitting. Those who didn't know Lanny personally—Sam, Helen, and Karen—attempted to start benign conversations. But the talk eventually gravitated back to the picker, and Jeff and Blanche answered as many questions as they could.

"What do you really know about this guy?" asked Karen.

"Enough," Jeff said.

"What's his last name?" asked Helen.

Jeff and Blanche exchanged glances. Her expression told him that she knew what he'd learned only hours before. "He . . ." Jeff debated his approach, decided to go with words pretty much from the horse's mouth. "He's paranoid about identity theft, so he keeps it close to the vest. And, you know, he probably has a good point. Have you ever noticed how naïve people are? Most give a lot more pertinent information than they need to."

Sheila said, "I've noticed that in the scrapbooking magazines." She added, "I subscribe to a few for greeting card ideas. Anyway, you can easily figure out from the journaling on the layouts where some of their regular contributors live and shop, what their children's names are, and where they attend school."

"True," Helen said, "but don't you think that those of you who are, or have been, involved in law enforcement get a little too paranoid when you look at Jane Homemaker? I love your cards, by the way, and I've seen those magazines: Two of my daughters have been published in them. Still, one can't get so distrustful that one doesn't enjoy life. Look how guarded you've been, and yet you were—" Helen's eyes grew wide. "Oh, Sheila, I'm so sorry. I didn't mean to—"

"Don't apologize, Helen, I'm fine. But you have a point, which leads me back to Lanny. If it weren't for him, I might not be fine. So, I'll try to respect his wishes, and Jeff can let him know that we're here if he needs us."

"What about you, Blanche?" Karen said. "You write him checks, don't you?"

Clearly the mercenary of the family, Jeff thought.

Blanche smiled. "No, actually. Lanny's my only cash-only, as it were. He says he doesn't trust banks."

"Well, he must have a last name. I mean, social security, income taxes, driver's license, car tags, insurance. He drives, doesn't he?"

"Yeah, that beat-up old truck."

"He sounds so . . . eccentric," said Helen. "I wonder what's behind it?"

"I think it's appealing," said Trudy. "I must admit, though, I've wondered what he's really like, behind his near-invisible existence."

"You know," Blanche said, "when I asked if he'd con- tacted a bondsman, he said they wouldn't let him go any- way."

"Why?" said Helen. "Do they have unquestionable proof that he killed someone?"

"He said he didn't kill anyone, and I believe him. He said, 'Because I told them my name's John Smith.' "

"Maybe he's in Witness Protection!" Karen was always looking for excitement.

"If that were true," Gordy said, "he'd have his ID so nailed down you couldn't budge it with a crowbar."

"Lots of people are named John Smith," Trudy said. "They can't hold him for that."

Sam grunted. "When someone who, for all appear- ances, seems to be homeless, the cops *don't* like to hear him say his name's John Smith."

Blanche said, "I like to believe that Lanny's thought of more as the old geezer in a small town. Everybody accepts him as a fixture, a part of the scenery. They don't question what he does, so long as it doesn't have a direct or negative effect on them, and they don't question who he is or what he's like because they regard him as a simpleton. Bottom line: They probably don't even *see* him, and that's exactly how he wants it."

"You've nailed it, Blanche," Jeff said. "All of that's probably true."

"But what if it's not?" Trudy said.

Jeff said, "Then this story is far from over."

Four

❦

AFTER THE PARTY, Jeff drove toward the jail in downtown Seattle and thought about the majolica pottery that was, apparently, not to be.

As was typical with their tendency to layer to the point of obsession, the Victorians were also obsessed with flowers and nature. To use a majolica jardiniere fashioned like a bouquet of flowers to hold a bouquet of flowers, or an oyster plate with wells shaped like a ring of open half-shells upon which to serve oysters on the half-shell was par for the course.

What Lanny had found (and had provided Jeff with a photo of earlier that day) was no different. The set consisted of two pieces: a large turtle that served as a water receptacle, designed to hang with its belly against the wall and its mouth open above a basin fashioned in the form of a lily pad. A spigot under the turtle's chin controlled the water's flow.

Lovers of the lead-glazed pottery would call it bright, cheerful, whimsical, and Jeff had immediately seen Sheila's reaction as just that. So, even though he didn't care much for the garish stuff, he—in the interest of making his wife happy—was as obsessed as the next collector when it came to tracking it down.

The turtle and lily pad set was perfect for the conservatory in many ways, and the more Jeff thought about losing out on it, the more upset he got. He hadn't realized till just now how set he'd been on acquiring it this weekend. And he knew that, if this particular deal fell through, he'd start putting out feelers for one just like it: contact the American Majolica Society, call Leila Dunbar at Sotheby's to personally check any majolica collections coming up on the auction block, track down dealers—like the guy in Indiana, for instance—who held regular majolica auctions.

And so it was that obsession wormed its way in. Frankly, Jeff was surprised that *more* people weren't killed over antiques.

He thought about what little he knew of majolica's American roots. When European majolica made such a splash at the 1876 Centennial Exposition in Philadelphia, American potters scrambled to cash in on its popularity. But they quickly learned that originality was not their key to success. The American consumers wanted exactly what they'd seen in the exhibitions from France and England. They wanted everything that the advances in technology, industry, and science offered. They wanted shell compotes supported by dolphin bases, and strawberry servers shaped like fruit-laden strawberry plants, and sardine boxes with lids sporting large sardine finials. So, the American potters, quite simply, stole the European designs. Their justification? Survival.

Survival. Likely, that was the only thing on Lanny's mind when he'd made a deal with Fiona for the majolica, and, just as likely, survival was all that was on his mind now.

It consumed Jeff's mind, too, as he wondered if he could help Lanny, wondered how the young man was holding up under the pressure—wondered how he himself had been able to enjoy a gourmet meal while someone who meant so much to him and Sheila sat in a cell. Waiting. At the King County jail downtown, Jeff went through the motions of showing ID, proving he had no weapon, and stating his business—hoping that his urgency wouldn't set off the metal detector. Miraculously, he was processed without so much as a hiccup, and was directed to the holding area.

The guard walked up to the cell. "John Smith," he said in a tone that confirmed he'd had his fill of aliases, "you got a visitor."

Several inmates turned their heads toward Jeff and the guard, and Jeff wondered how many had the alias, had used the alias, or wished they could now steal the alias.

One inmate catcalled, "Smith, your boyfriend's too old for you but he sure do dress pretty." He laughed heartily at his own joke. Lanny ignored him.

Jeff had forgotten he was wearing a tux. Thank God he'd left the cape behind. "You okay?" he said to Lanny through the bars.

"Blanche was supposed to tell you not to come."

"She mentioned it but I just thought you didn't want to inconvenience anybody. I waited till we were through eating." *Lame.*

The guard unlocked the cell, then escorted Lanny and Jeff to a conference room. They seated themselves across the table from each other. Jeff watched the guard pull the door shut behind him before speaking.

"Lanny, did you kill Fiona? I mean, if you did, tell me now and we'll figure out where to go from here."

The hurt in Lanny's eyes made Jeff feel like a heel. Lanny clenched his jaw. "I'm not a killer."

"I believe you. I just needed to hear it. Understand?"

"I did not kill Fiona Brock."

"The cops will need more than your word, though."

"Then let them find it out for themselves."

"Don't you understand? They aren't going to look if they take your silence as guilt."

Lanny stole a glance at Jeff, looked back down.

Jeff hated to lay the next card on the table but you had to play what you were dealt. "At least tell me, since you were working for me today, what happened?"

It was obvious from Lanny's expression that he hadn't thought of it from that angle. He'd been paid by Jeff to acquire a piece of majolica and, in the course of doing that, the majolica had been sold to someone else and the seller had been murdered. "Your money's in my bank account. I'll get it for you as soon as—"

"I'm not worried about the money, Lanny. How'd you end up here?"

Lanny put his elbows on the table, then removed them just as quickly. He sat back, folded his arms across his chest. "I went back to Fiona's shop to get the turtle set for you and another piece of majolica for . . . someone else. Fiona was—" he paused, rubbed his eyes as if he were trying to erase an image—"she wasn't up front. I called to her a few times, looked around as I walked through the shop. The longer I was in there, the more I thought how anyone could just step in from the street, see that no one was around, and grab something. I yelled out for her then, and went toward the back room." He shuddered slightly. "That's when I found her."

"Where was she, exactly?"

"Seated at her desk, slumped over a book about majolica. I think it was a clue. At first, I thought she'd fallen asleep. Then, I considered the fact that she might have had a heart attack. I went closer to check for a pulse. That's when I saw the blood."

"Blood?"

"Not much. On the back of her neck."

Likely, a single blow killed her, Jeff thought. "What then?"

"What do you think? I called for an ambulance."

"Did you wait for it to arrive?"

"Sure. Cops, too."

"Did they arrest you when they got there?"

"Not at first. But when they asked things like, did I know the victim, and when was the last time I'd spoken with her, I was straightforward about everything. I told them we'd had words this afternoon. That's when they brought me down here."

"You and Fiona argued?"

"Yeah. When I went back to buy the stuff."

"You were at her shop three times today?"

"Right. This morning, when I found the pieces, then this afternoon, when I went back with the money to buy them, and at closing, when I found her . . . when I found her at her desk."

"Why'd you go back a third time if she had already sold the stuff you wanted?"

Lanny lifted a shoulder. "To try to set things right, I guess. I mean, I know that she's struggling—*was* struggling—like the rest of us. After I cooled off, I went back to apologize, to tell her I understood. And, I was going to ask her to keep an eye out for more majolica. Anyway, that's when I found her."

"Obviously," Jeff said, "there wasn't anyone else there."

"Do you think I'd be here if there had been?"

"Sorry, just thinking out loud. What about the second time, when you went there to buy the majolica? Anyone hear you argue?"

Lanny grunted. "There's always a witness when you don't need one. I had five."

"Did you know any of them? Did you give their names to the police?"

"What do you think? I'm not trying to hide anything. If

I were, I wouldn't have hung around after I called nine-one-one."

Good point. "Okay, what time was the first visit?"

"When she opened. Ten o'clock."

"Was anyone else around who might've heard her promise to hold the majolica?"

"Yeah. Two other pickers were at the back. One of them had already rung the back bell. Fiona was out of breath when she reached the door, said she had three customers waiting at the front door when she arrived."

"As I recall, she always gets there early."

"Yeah. She wants plenty of time to warm up some milk for Dry Rot—that's the shop cat—and to make tea for herself."

Jeff was constantly amazed at the predilection for antiques shops and mystery bookstores to house finicky felines. Jeff could always tell when he'd entered the abode of a cat because his nose itched. It itched now, just at the thought, and he sawed at the region above his upper lip with a knuckle. "I haven't been to her shop in ages. For all her impatience with people, she sure doted over that cat."

Lanny smiled slightly. "She did that. This morning, though, she said that when she first arrived and opened the door, Dry Rot shot out of the shop like someone had singed his tail. She always worried that he'd bolt like that. He had never set foot outside before today."

"What about visits to the vet? Shots and all that?"

"Oh, she used a pet carrier for that. I helped her load it into her van once."

"Did she find the cat this morning?"

"I did, actually. I'd seen him dart down a dead-end alley, and had tried to catch him. When I couldn't, I got a can of kitty treats from Fiona. She always wore one of those oversized sweater-coats, with a can of treats sticking up out of the right pocket and a bottle of Tums sticking out of the left one. Anyway, I took the can and lured Dry Rot out of his hiding place with a handful of treats. Then I latched onto him and got him back to the shop."

"I wonder what would've made him leave like that?"

"You know cats."

Jeff didn't but he nodded. He also made a mental note that Fiona seemed to have trusted Lanny.

"I remember the one I had as a kid—called him Graves, after—" Lanny interrupted himself. "Anyway, they don't think like other animals."

Jeff thought it would take a lot to spook a black shop cat, especially so close to Halloween. Weren't they in stalking mode or something? "She must've appreciated your help."

"I thought so, too. Funny way of showing it, though, by selling those pieces out from under me."

"Could she have gotten *that* much more money from someone else?"

"Possibly, if the buyer wanted them bad enough. But they weren't over-the-top valuable, you know? Nothing really rare."

"Had she just acquired them?"

"The night before. Why?"

"Maybe it was a misunderstanding. You know, the wife says to the husband, 'Haul away these boxes,' and he picks up a box that wasn't meant to go, and the wife tells him to get back her grandmother's collection, or she's going to kill him. Something like that."

Lanny seemed deep in thought for several seconds before he said, "You could be right. If so, then maybe the husband paid a lot more than he'd originally gotten for the stuff, just to get his wife off his back."

Jeff nodded agreement. "Sometimes, it's the best bargain you'll ever make."

FIVE

❦

*T*HEY SAT IN silence for awhile, Jeff giving Lanny some space. Hopefully, the young picker was organizing his thoughts, allowing information to drop into mental slots, searching for anything that might help. Jeff stood, paced the room. "What happened then, after you'd gotten the cat back?"

Lanny sighed, as if he'd been holding his breath, and rubbed his eyes. "Fiona juggled customers and pickers while she coddled the cat, who was kind of twitchy and knocked over two vases before she got him settled down. He lapped up his milk, finally, then curled up in his bed under Fiona's desk."

"A few years ago," Jeff said, "I read about a cat that knocked over a majolica cat—and knocked its value from twenty-five grand down to ten after all was said and done."

"It still brought ten thousand dollars?"

"Yep. Professional restorers."

Lanny nodded.

Jeff debated where to start. "Did you know any of the customers from your first visit there this morning?"

"No, and the other pickers left before Fiona and I agreed on a price for the majolica. In other words, no one to back my story that she was going to sell the stuff to me."

Jeff stood. "Any chance Fiona had surveillance cameras?"

"Three of them. She kept a sharp eye on the monitors, too."

Most antiques shopkeepers—even the ones running junkers—had invested in surveillance equipment. A thought came to Jeff. "Recording?"

"Yeah, but not in the office area in back, and not twenty-four/seven. I thought of that, too. She turned it off at quitting time before setting the entry alarm. And she always shunted the motion detectors because of Dry Rot." Lanny leaned forward. "Maybe whoever killed her didn't think that far ahead, didn't know about the cameras."

"I hope you're right." Jeff knew that, at that very moment, the tapes were probably serving as some detective's Saturday night movie. "She left the cat downstairs?"

"She left the upstairs door open. That way, Dry Rot could roam."

Jeff had forgotten that the woman lived upstairs. He thought he was getting the picture, though: The victim and the accused had a close relationship. Fiona was Lanny's bread and butter, much like Blanche was Jeff's. Or, had been, before Sheila had started up their eBay store.

Jeff wondered how all of this would affect Lanny financially. Fiona's death might actually push the guy to find another line of work, but Jeff couldn't picture Lanny doing anything else. And, till this moment, Jeff hadn't even thought about the pay cut Lanny had taken when Jeff left the FBI to go into antiques. Unless, of course, Lanny was now someone else's informant. Jeff knew better than to ask.

"Fiona stayed open through lunch, right?"

"Right. There's an old Coldspot fridge in the back, one of those short ones with the rounded corners. She usually had it stocked with sandwich stuff. She used to go up to her apartment for lunch, but the climb was too much when her arthritis got worse. She only made the trip upstairs after closing shop every day."

"Listen," Jeff said. "What do you need me to do?"

Another shrug. "Nothing you can do. I'm not giving them my life story. Besides, it's Saturday night. Since I can't get an arraignment till Monday morning, I'm trying to look at this as a wise business move. Three squares, free hot water, a workout program. Just like working for Microsoft."

The statement was delivered with a heavy dose of sarcasm, something Jeff wasn't used to hearing from Lanny.

"Do you need anything from home? I don't know what they'll let you have, but . . . "

"I've already got that covered. Tom Walcher, a buddy of mine, works in the building where I stay."

"How'd he know you were here? Last I heard, they were only allowing one phone call, and you used that to call my house."

Lanny said, "A gal I know saw them haul me in, told Tom. He's already been here and gone."

Jeff blinked. Could he call himself a real friend? If so, why hadn't he responded like this Tom guy had—drop everything, jump in and help. Until this situation, he hadn't considered Lanny's life beyond how it directly related to his own. When he was an agent, he blocked any curiosity about his informants. It was better that way. Since then, though, he'd never wondered whether Lanny had a family, or friends, or a girlfriend. "You know, Lanny, I . . . I want to help. I just don't know what to offer."

"Just keep your ears open in case any info turns up

about the majolica I was trying to get for you. I need to know who Fiona sold it to."

"Sure, but you realize, don't you, that this was likely a random act? The majolica probably has nothing to do with it." He debated telling Lanny what Blanche—and all the other dealers—thought of the victim but decided against it. And, as far as the majolica went, finding the buyer wouldn't do any good. Someone who'd pay enough to persuade Fiona to break her deal with Lanny wasn't going to be turning the merchandise anytime soon.

"It's clear that she sold the majolica to someone else. Therefore, that person had no reason to come back and kill her. I don't see how the majolica plays into the picture."

"What if I'm not the only one she had promised it to?"

Before Jeff had a chance to point out the ridiculousness of that question, Lanny waved him off. "I know, I know. It wasn't there, so she obviously dealt with someone else. Don't pay attention to what I say. I'm just spitting out what comes to mind."

"That's smart. It could be your ticket out of here."

Lanny said, "Look. I already told the detective everything. He said they'd try to track down everyone, check the surveillance tapes, all that. What do you want, proof that I fought with Fiona? Believe me, they've got that."

Lanny was right. The more people who could claim that they'd witnessed the argument, the more trouble Lanny was in. Jeff held up a palm. "Like I said before, the thing about prosecutors is they aren't going to look past you for this unless we can give them sound reason to."

Lanny didn't respond.

Jeff sighed. "Okay. Spend your time here going over everything, every detail, no matter how trivial it might seem. With your permission, I'll go with you to your arraignment on Monday. Maybe we can convince the judge you're trustworthy, get him or her to release you on your own recognizance, if I vouch for you. Hard to say, since this is a murder charge, but I think we should try."

"Why stick your neck out for me?"

"You say you didn't kill her. You've never lied to me before. My life depended on my trusting you when I was an agent, and I doubt your ethics have changed since then."

"I'll say it as many times as I have to: She was already dead when I got there."

"It won't hurt for me to poke around tomorrow, see if anyone has some majolica for sale." He felt it was the least he could do, since the guy was stuck behind bars. "What am I looking for?"

"I gave you the photo, right?"

"For the turtle set," Jeff said, "but what about the other piece?"

Lanny stood. "I'm done messing with this. If you find any good-quality majolica, have the seller hold it till you reach me."

"Yeah, right, Lanny. That worked so well for you before, didn't it?"

Jeff had seen it before: His statement hit Lanny square between the eyes, changed only the pupils but changed them visibly.

The guard opened the door, and informed the pair that their time was up. The prisoner left without further comment.

SIX

NOISES WOKE JEFF, something he wasn't used to most mornings, particularly on Sundays. The usually quiet house was lively with laughter from Karen and Gordy, tings of metal against glass as Sheila whipped up breakfast, doors shutting here and there throughout the house, and squawking coming from the conservatory. At least, he hoped that's where it was coming from.

He pulled on gray track pants and a sweatshirt from his UDub alma mater (also gray, with a purple husky on the front under an arced "Washington"), then followed his nose down to the coffeepot.

Everything and everyone was in motion. Greer carried a silver tray laden with half-full dishes of jellies, honey, butter, and strawberry cream cheese from the breakfast nook and placed it on the counter beside the refrigerator. Gordy poured the last of the coffee into a mug and handed it to Jeff. Greer started a fresh pot, then left the room. Sheila and Karen chatted over a large picnic basket Sheila was stocking from a stash of variously wrapped packages and plastic containers gathered on the long refectory table. Karen snapped digital shots of her sister. Both wore jeans and tucked-in white shirts, but Sheila wore loafers and no belt while Karen wore retro cowboy boots and a concho belt.

Jeff siphoned off an inch of the strong, hot liquid, then said, "Breakfast?"

Sheila said, "Do you want breakfast now? You usually need a few cups of coffee first."

"I'll wait."

"I'll fix you up a plate as soon as I'm through here. Gordy and Karen have to get going, so we went ahead and ate."

Jeff nodded. He'd had a nightcap with Gordy the night before and had filled him in on the visit with Lanny. Gordy had mentioned then that he had to leave early.

"How's your friend?" Karen swiped a miniature quiche from a serving tray on the range-top and popped it into her mouth.

"Hanging in there. He can't get an arraignment till tomorrow morning."

"Did he do it?" Karen's tone was innocuous.

"No." Jeff waited for someone to question him but everyone was quiet. He watched Sheila expertly pack more things into the basket. Since he knew full well that she wasn't about to leave for a picnic, he said, "What's going on?"

"Karen has her camper, of course, so I'm fixing up a care package for the road."

Jeff had noticed the vintage podlike camper with its retro airbrushed paintings on the sides when he'd returned from the jail the night before. It hadn't been there before dinner. "Where did you hide that thing yesterday?"

"At Greer's friend Robbie's place. Greet arranged it

ahead of time. When I pulled into Seattle yesterday, I headed straight over there. Robbie gave me a lift here yesterday afternoon. I went back over to get my wheels last night, after you'd gone down to the police station."

"You mean, you were here when I came by with Lanny?"

"Sure was." She flashed a conspiratorial smile at her sister, got one in return.

"Huh," Jeff grunted. "I didn't think you could keep quiet for that long."

"Ha, ha," his sister-in-law said flatly. "For your information, I was upstairs grabbing a nap."

"Me, too," said Gordy. He sat at the far end of the table, absently thumbing through a book on training parrots. "I knew that the time change would screw me up during the party, and I've been working day and night on a case. My rental car was hidden at Robbie's, too."

"And I," Karen said, "had finished a two-day drive from Cody, Wyoming, after leaving behind one of the cutest cowboys ever to wear a hat, just to help you turn forty. So, if you don't be good to your favorite sister-in-law—"

"Only sister-in-law."

"Which means, of course, that I'm your fave. As I was saying, if you don't be good to me, I won't sell you the loot I brought up from the Indians."

"Indians?" She had his attention.

"Indians. I helped a Navajo family when they were in a car accident while I was working in Arizona. They were so grateful they insisted on giving me a bunch of old turquoise jewelry, some pottery that they wrapped up in woven rugs and blankets, that kind of stuff. I told them that all I wanted was permission to photograph them. They gave it but still insisted that I take the items."

Jeff said, "That's macabre, Karen."

"What?" she said before realization filled her face. "Oh, come on. They weren't injured, just stranded." She grabbed a small portfolio from next to her backpack propped near the door and handed it to him.

He zipped open the folder and looked into some of the most amazing eyes he'd ever seen. The boy couldn't have been more than four or five years old, yet his gaze was so intense, so intelligent.

"He has an old soul, don't you think?" Karen said.

"You're right." Jeff flipped through the other sepia-tone shots, amazed at the character Karen had captured in each of her subjects: the teenaged girls who couldn't keep from grinning; the parents, their expressions a layer of fear and struggle, yet independence and pride, as well.

"I don't know what you get paid, Karen, but it's not enough."

"Why, Jeff, I believe that's the first compliment you've ever paid me."

"That's not true," Sheila said. "He always praises the photos you send me."

Jeff said, "I told you that last night."

"I don't remember it. Was I drinking at the time?" She grinned mischievously.

Jeff zipped the folder and returned it to his sister-in-law, then twisted in his chair and took a couple of the quiches. "So," he said around a bite, "where's the stuff?"

"Out in the camper. We have time for more coffee, though."

Gordy filled everyone's cups from the freshly brewed pot.

"Where's Greer?" Jeff asked.

Karen said, "I asked him to bring my duffel bag down but you know Greer. By now, he has all the beds on the second floor stripped and done up with fresh sheets. He—"

Just then, Greer passed through the kitchen, duffel bag in hand.

Karen seemed embarrassed. Jeff considered marking the calendar but hated to chance undoing the goodwill he'd gained by complimenting her photos. He might need to draw on it when they commenced negotiations for the loot.

"Thank you, Greer," Sheila said.

"Yes, ma'am. Everything on the second floor is in order."

After he'd walked out the door, Karen said, "I feel like I've been caught gossiping."

"You were," Jeff said.

Sheila gave him a warning look.

He shrugged innocently.

Karen, obviously clueless, continued. "I mean, I know he's a lot of help but how is it you don't feel like he's, I don't know, spying or something? It'd freak me out, never having time completely alone."

"We don't have time for me to explain it to you," Sheila said as she peeked out the window over the sink. "Now, about that Native American stuff: How can you so easily get rid of everything they gave you as a gesture of appreciation?"

Jeff chuckled. "Aren't you forgetting who you're talking to, hon? Miss Streamline made a major commitment when she bought that camper. It's probably the most square footage she's ever owned. Thanks to people like her, we make a living." *In other words,* Jeff thought, *don't jinx this deal.*

Greer walked back through the kitchen, seized a large tray filled with serving dishes, and kept moving.

"Jeff's right, Sis," Karen said. "I'm keeping a few things because they look great in the camper. I don't have the space for more than that."

Gordy swigged coffee, glanced at his watch. "Gotta get back to Chicago. Sheila"—he enveloped her in one of his bear hugs—"I had a great time. Thanks again."

"Buddy," he said, slapping Jeff on the back, "stay in touch."

"Will do." It was still their code, after all these years. This time it meant, *Let me know what happens with Lanny.*

Gordy and Karen exchanged a quick farewell, and then he was gone.

Karen said, "Canada calls. We should bring in that stuff if you want a look."

Jeff followed her outside, where the camper and Karen's heavy-duty pickup were backed into the driveway. He had to admit that it was a cool-looking package: the pickup truck and little camper with their two-tone paint jobs in maroon and khaki, and the camper's airbrushed montage of sepia photos depicting scenes from days gone by: everything from rodeos to state fairs, Victorian portraits to sharecroppers. The sides read "Gray's Photo Emporium," in an arc of elaborately scrolled letters that put one in mind of nineteenth-century itinerants selling snake oil and liniment. Below that, in simple block letters: KAREN GRAY, FREELANCE PHOTOGRAPHY.

"I didn't see these details last night. This looks amazing."

Karen waved him off. "Another one of my phases, I'm sure. When I get tired of it, I'll move on to something else."

Jeff shook his head. "I want first dibs on this camper."

With Sheila's help locating vintage fabrics and accessories, Karen had created a dude ranch on wheels. The interior of the old trailer was done up with bandana paisleys, blue denim, faux paint-pony hide, and the retro print of pinup cowgirls perched on fences, and standing beside watering troughs and cacti. The complementary mix of patterns and colors instantly evoked a warm nostalgia, and Jeff wondered why Westerns weren't more popular with the general public. Who hadn't wanted to be a cowboy or a cowgirl at one time or another?

A stack of Indian blankets at one end of the banquette, that clearly served as a couch during the day and a bed at night, was cinched with a tooled leather belt. The belt closed with a buckle that held a chunk of brown-veined turquoise large enough to choke a horse.

"Is that for sale?"

"No way. It looks too good there, don't you think?"

Jeff stifled a sigh. That single bundle was worth thousands.

"Don't worry," Karen said as she pulled a two-by-four-foot lidded plastic storage container from atop the built-in table. "I've got enough loot to make the Talbots plenty happy. Let's take this inside so Sheila can handpick some pieces for her eBay store. Being an online seller has done her more good than I ever would've imagined."

Jeff hoisted the container, squeezed it through the narrow door. "Yeah, she loves what she's doing. She's busier than I've ever seen her."

"Between the antiques and the conservatory, I can imagine. That was a surprise, by the way. I can't believe she bought birds."

"Neither can I. They're driving me nuts."

"Don't worry. She'll come to her senses."

Jeff wasn't sure what Karen was basing her prediction on but he hoped she was right.

Inside, Sheila had cleared everything from the seven-foot-long refectory table. While Karen unpacked the container onto the table's surface, Jeff and Sheila grabbed notepads and pens.

The three of them were in the same gotta-get-moving mode, so the process was quick and painless.

Jeff and Sheila purchased the lot, which included three area rugs, two blankets, several pieces of silver and turquoise jewelry (cuff bracelets, rings, earrings, and an amazing squash blossom necklace), and a long, narrow beaded bag that Jeff identified as a tobacco pouch. When he crunched numbers and showed the figure to Karen, she halved it, claiming the bargain as her contribution to Sheila's new career. "Besides," she said, "that's enough to keep me in food for quite awhile—in case this photography thing doesn't work out." She grinned.

Sheila's eyes glittered. "Well, I know what I'm doing this afternoon."

Jeff said, "Do you think we should check with Blanche before you list all of it on-line?"

"Oh, Blanche won't want it," Karen said, surprising Jeff. "She overheard me mention it to Sheila last night, before you came downstairs."

"Why am I even in on this, then?" Jeff asked.

"We have to make you feel needed." Karen looked at him innocently.

Sheila said, "I do need him. He's the one who knows what to pay for stuff. I'm better at marketing it so that it makes a decent profit on-line."

"I can take a hint," Jeff said as he walked out of the kitchen. "I'll be back with a check."

When he returned, Karen grabbed the check and her sister simultaneously. After the embrace, she said, "Gotta run. I want to get these northern assignments finished quickly so I can head south for the winter."

She gave Jeff a quick hug, and flew out the door.

And that was how visits from Karen usually were, leaving heads bobbing in her wake.

"That girl," Sheila said, shaking her head and seemingly forgetting that Karen was the older of the two. Jeff expected more to the sentence but Sheila let it drop, grabbed the plastic tub full of loot, and started up the stairs.

"Hey." Jeff caught up to her, took the load, and followed her up to her office. "Do we have the right books for checking the value of this stuff?"

"Jeff, give me a little credit."

"It's not that. I mean, some of this might be museum quality."

"You're kidding. Why didn't you tell Karen?"

"Because it wouldn't have mattered."

"That's true, I suppose." Sheila studied the container. "What do you want me to do?"

"Try to nail some of it down before you start listing it.

I've been playing phone tag with Lee Dunbar all week about those old jack-o'-lanterns, so I can ask her who might be interested in some high-quality Native American artifacts."

He didn't think the majolica was crucial but he might as well play along, show support for Lanny and, at the same time, do some picking for himself. That way, it wouldn't be a total waste of time, and he could honestly say that he was helping Lanny by doing what he asked. He said, "I'm going over to the Fremont Market later."

Sheila turned. "What? You're working on a Sunday?"

He smiled. "Isn't that what you're doing?"

"I . . . but . . . Jeff Talbot, this is different and you know it."

"Just joking, hon. I'm nosing around for some info that might help Lanny."

"Good. If I can do anything to help, let me know."

He hesitated at first, unsure whether to tell her about the gift he'd been trying to get for her through Lanny. Now, though, he realized that surprising her took backseat to a man's freedom. He gave her the main points of the story, then retrieved the photo of the set from his dressing room.

"Oh, Jeff, you're trying to get this for my conservatory? It's incredible. Thank you." She hugged him.

"Don't get your hopes up. It may not surface again in our lifetimes. Then again, it might not hurt to check on-line for the set. Maybe Lanny's right, and Fiona's murder is somehow tied to the deal he'd made with her."

Sheila glanced at the photo. "Surely Lanny told the detectives that. Won't they be looking for them on-line?"

"You'd think so. But I suspect they're concentrating more on finding the murder weapon. If they *are* searching for the merchandise, though, it might help Lanny if we found the stuff first."

"How's that going to help?"

"It might lead to the killer, or to a witness, or to more

suspects. I don't know. It could even tell us if there's some-thing else going on, or—"

"Okay, okay. Too many variables." She kissed him, then waggled the photo. "Thanks again for trying to get this for me. I'll keep an eye out for it in the electronic world."

As Jeff headed for the shower, he wondered whether Lanny was right to suspect that the majolica had some-thing to do with Fiona's murder. What if it did, though, and the cops weren't even bothering to look for it? Jeff wasn't sure which was worse.

SEVEN

❦

$\mathcal{T}$HE DRIVE FROM Jeff's home in upscale Queen Anne to funky Fremont was ten minutes and two planets away.

The community's official motto, *De Libertas Quirkas* (Freedom to Be Peculiar) was displayed on a fifty-three-foot rocket left over from the Cold War.

Jeff parked along the ship canal near the Adobe Systems building and Gas Works Park, and walked toward the center of town. The weather threatened rain, and the wind was sharp enough to slice bread on, but it hadn't cut market attendance.

Even a few bicyclists were out, taking advantage of the Burke-Gilman Trail that paralleled an abandoned Burlington Northern rail-bed.

He heard music, and the chattering noise from the crowds as he neared the market. It lifted his spirits. He would come up here more often, but it seemed different leaving Sheila on a weekend as opposed to the work week. Besides, one of their favorite things to do before she'd become housebound had been to attend the neighborhood's Outdoor Cinema, and bittersweet memories prevented his coming up here too often. The last film they'd seen here was *Casablanca,* and they had retired it to that memory, vowing never to watch it again.

Jeff thought the neighborhood motto could just as easily be "Freedom to Express Yourself," because of all the altered art he saw as he strolled through the makeshift aisles of tables holding wares that ranged from jewelry to junk, vegetables to vases, apples to accordions. Whether it was the Garden of Everyday Miracles (where he counted—among other things—fourteen plastic pink flamingos, three dead microwaves, and a macramé owl) or the Halloween costumes that currently adorned the "People Waiting for the Interurban" sculpture, Fremont meant freedom. As if to give weight to that policy, a mime practiced his (or her, Jeff wasn't sure) moves on the statue.

The bohemian neighborhood was also home to the Fremont Troll, a cement monstrosity that lived under the bridge and gripped a real VW Bug in its fist. Vandals once broke into its trunk, looking for treasure. As a treasure hunter himself, Jeff understood the temptation.

There was a certain colloquy among the residents of Fremont, which had resulted in harmony over the blue and orange paint job maintained on Fremont Bridge, the face of a former Fremont mayor on the cast aluminum dog in the People Waiting sculpture, and the seven-ton statue of Lenin that, last Jeff knew, was still for sale.

That was Fremont now. Jeff had heard much about the community's early history as a mill town from his lumber baron grandfather. The old man hated the citified direction Fremont was taking back before he died in 1988. No telling what he'd say about the place if he were alive now.

Jeff used his Libra sensibilities as he browsed, focusing his attention on pottery yet keeping an eye out for any and all bargains. He found a small collection of Rookwood, and the matte greens and browns appealed to him but, by his estimation, the pieces were overpriced. A few cookie jars and small planters turned out to be Shawnee knock-offs. Brightly colored rooster figurines were everywhere, and the Chanticleer's image graced everything from potholders and dinnerware to lampshades and throw pillows.

But Jeff found no majolica.

He bought a few things he could turn for a profit: old postcards, a spindle with a sheaf of receipts—1940s era—still skewered on it, and an elaborately scrolled iron stand shaped like a rectangular trough in which to cradle a bicycle tire. Jeff supposed the vendor didn't know what it was, or he could have advertised it as a hot item for the bicyclists of the community.

Finally, he bought a Suffragette brooch. It was unmarked, and, again, he suspected the seller didn't know the controversial history behind the jewelry with its green, white, and violet stones. The initials GWV are said to stand for *Give Women the Vote,* and jewelers used peridot (green), pearl or moonstone (white), and amethyst (violet) to represent the petition. It's said by some that women used it to identify one another as sisters of the cause. Others now claim it's a hoax. Either way, Jeff saw it as an appealing collectible and a token of history.

Sheila had asked Jeff to keep an eye out for clothes that might serve as Halloween costumes, and there was no better place than the home of Trolloween to dig up something fitting. He had put up his annual fuss over having to dress up for the little hobgoblins but, as usual, had caved in at Sheila's insistence. He was sure she knew—although he'd never admit to it—that he enjoyed the evening once things got underway. Even Greer, who had a ready-made costume in his butler's attire, changed things up a bit with vintage striped trousers and a gray waistcoat that had belonged to his butler grandfather. The return trick-or-treaters always asked after "Greer, the butler of the mansion," affecting their version of a British accent before giving way to fits of giggles. It was an encouraging sign, and Jeff hoped that today's kids were stealing from the sandman by way of flashlights and mystery novels, just as he had done while growing up.

Next, he poked around Deluxe Junk, then Fritzi Ritz, trying to find costumes, but nothing jumped out at him. He walked, perusing store windows for inspiration and, after awhile, shelved the chore. He made his way back around to his woodie, then swung over to Archie McPhee's and stocked up on plastic spiders and slugs before leaving the street fair behind him.

He rolled down to Seattle proper, and popped into a Tully's for coffee. Everyone in the coffee shop seemed happier than usual, and he attributed this to the recent results of a vote on a proposed initiative to tax espresso and use the money to fund preschool programs. The idea had been thrown out like wet coffee grounds. Although Jeff didn't drink espresso, he nonetheless drank his garden-variety bean juice with more appreciation than usual.

He took his coffee and drank it as he walked toward the jail.

The general atmosphere was calmer than it had been the night before, but Lanny wasn't. He appeared to have gotten almost no sleep, and he jumped at every sound, every movement.

"I'm sorry we can't get you out of here," Jeff said.

"Luck of the draw. Any leads on the majolica?"

Jeff wondered why Lanny hadn't asked about leads on the murder. "No. Nothing yet."

Lanny dropped back against the chair.

Jeff said, "Nothing on Fiona's killer, either."

"You think I don't care. It's just that I think the majolica holds the answer."

"It could be anything, Lanny. Why are you still hung up on the majolica?"

"I don't know. Maybe it's because what she did was so out of character, even if she did need more money. And, don't give me that bit about some husband accidentally selling it. I've been thinking about that, and Fiona would've told me if that was what happened."

"Okay," Jeff said, "then what was it about the majolica that would make someone pay such an inflated amount that it would persuade her to break your deal?"

"I don't—" Lanny stopped.

Usually, his close-to-the-vest approach permeated everything about him: his stance, his expression—or *lack* of expression, Jeff corrected. But the tell that Jeff now saw in the man's eyes was unmistakable: the abrupt realization was too astounding to hide. Lanny looked as if that last hole card had lost him the game. Just as quickly, the poker face was back.

"What?" Jeff didn't expect an answer but he had to ask.

"Nothing."

Jeff knew better. "Lanny, I can't help you if you're not up front with me. Do you have an enemy you haven't told me about?"

"Why would you ask that?"

"You obviously thought of *something*. Fiona's dead, and items you were parlaying are gone. Does it have to do with you, instead of her?"

"I really don't know."

After a moment, Lanny continued. "You know better than anybody how careful I've been. You said yourself I was the best informant you'd ever seen. The type of life I lead, sure, I guess someone might have it out for me. Anybody who doesn't have his head in the sand could say the same thing, right? To answer your question, though: If someone's out to mess with me, I don't know who it'd be."

Jeff needed to take the conversation in another direction, for now. "Do you know whether Fiona had any relatives?"

"She said she didn't. Always said that if anything happened to her, she wanted an auction of the goods in the store. She'd cackle when she said that, said she'd be floating in the rafters so she could watch all the pickers scrambling for what was hers."

Jeff said, "That's the part of picking I'll never warm up to: the night-before campouts at estate sales, the low-rent tactics."

"You have to from time to time, though, if you're going to make a living at this."

"Yeah, and I'll admit, the time-to-times are getting more frequent as the treasures get more scarce—but I don't have to like it." Jeff slid down in his chair, stretched his legs out in front of him and crossed his ankles. "A week ago Friday, I actually had to break up a knock-down-dragout fight between a couple of pickers outside an Italianate in Portland. Sometimes, it makes me wonder why I left the FBI for this business. I was safer there."

"You do tend to stumble onto trouble more than any picker I've seen—and I've seen all kinds. At the same time, you have a knack for scoring big—like you'll do with all the stuff rumored to be in Frenchie the baker's house."

Jeff had mentioned Pierre "Frenchie" Hoffman to Lanny a few weeks earlier. "Yeah, well, I haven't heard back from him yet."

"Maybe you should call him."

"The secret of my success is knowing when not to push."

"Remember that when I don't want to answer your questions." Lanny repositioned himself in the uncomfortable-looking chair. "Maybe old Frenchie's ticker finally gave out. He might be in the hospital."

"That crossed my mind, too. I'll head down there if I don't hear from him next week. Now, speaking of questions, what about the people who heard you argue with Fiona yesterday? Do you want to tell me about them?"

In spite of the subject, Lanny smiled slightly. "I concede. You do get around to asking questions."

"You don't have to answer but it might help."

"No reason not to. I've got nothin' to do, and nothin' to hide." Lanny leaned back. "There was a couple—man and woman—trying to decide on a piece of jewelry. From the way they talked, they worked together and were on their lunch hour. She was trying to help him get something for his wife's birthday. He mentioned that she liked old amethyst and marcasite."

"Fiona has estate jewelry, stuff like that?"

"Yeah. The shop looks junked-up, but it's just because she tries to cram so much into a small space. She always knew exactly what she had, though, and where it was."

"The cops might be able to find the pair, but it'll take a lot of work. Who else?"

"Tom was there."

"The guy who was here last night? Wachler?"

"It's Walcher. Yeah. I'd told him that Fiona had a bunch of paperback mysteries. I would've picked them up for him but he reads so many I wouldn't have known what to get."

"Maybe we should put him on this case."

"What makes you think I haven't? Anyway, he'd dropped by to go through the paperbacks. Sally was giving him a hard time for—"

"Sally?"

"Yeah, Mustang Sally. Haven't you heard about her?"

"No but let me guess: Her name's Sally and she drives a Mustang."

"She says her name's Sally. I've never questioned her about it. You can't miss her. Six-feet-two, natural platinum blonde, pretty, in a heroin-chic sort of way."

"Sounds like she should be a supermodel."

"She was, till she got hooked on crack trying to stay skeletal. Traded the vintage Mustang one night for a fix. Fast-forward to post-rehab. She hoboed her way from New

York to Seattle on Amtrak, says someone on the train gave her the nickname."

"You mean she didn't get the name till after she'd lost the car?"

"Ironic, isn't it? Remember in school how you'd always want a cool nickname, but you got stuck with Stinky or Wart Face or something lame like that?"

"Yeah."

"Yeah." Lanny seemed lost in thought for a moment. "Anyway, Sally got real nervous-like when Fiona started yelling. She's already kind of high-strung. But she was holding a camel-colored vintage coat that she wanted to buy—winter on the streets, you know—and it was like she wasn't gonna leave without that coat. Tom had an arm-load of the paperbacks and was waiting at the register. He knows how things are with Sally, so he glanced at the ticket on the coat, slapped a couple of twenties on the counter, and told Fiona that he and Sally would catch her next time."

"At those prices, I should've shopped there more often."

"The coat was marked down. Not many gals around built like Sally."

"Good point. Who else was there?"

Lanny looked up at the ceiling as if it were a projector screen for his memory, then looked back at Jeff. "There was some other guy at the front of the shop. Fiona kept glancing at him. I remember wondering whether she thought he was trying to steal something, or whether she was irritated that the argument might scare a customer away."

"Did you notice what he looked like?"

"Average, I guess. Struck me as clean-cut. Wore all dark blue—ball cap, windbreaker, jeans."

"When did—"

"Wait . . . yeah, I remember now." Lanny closed his eyes and as he spoke, his hands mimicked the movements he relayed. "That guy picked up something . . . a celestial globe that was on an old dresser . . . open construction, with a small earth in the center, and a band forming a larger circle around the earth." He opened his eyes. "It had astrological markings on it."

"I've seen them but I don't know how to use them."

Lanny looked away again, stared at a spot on the floor. "He turned it over to check for any markings. I'd seen the globe before—it's been in the shop for over a month. I could tell first time I saw it that it was a repro, nineteen-sixties, instead of the seventeen-sixties. The pedestal base looked like real wood but when you took a closer look, you could see that it was some sort of composite."

"If it's still there . . ."

"Then the cops can dust it for prints! Should be easy on that base."

Jeff had never seen Lanny this excited. He hated to squelch it, but . . . "You realize this means they can track down another witness to the fight. That might hurt instead of help."

A flicker of despair shone in Lanny's eyes. "Do you think there's any way to get the cops to check for prints on the globe's base without telling them why?"

"Hard to say, but we can try. On the other hand, what if he's . . . like Sally, for instance. This is a stretch, but maybe he's on the street, trying to make ends meet, whatever—and he commiserated with you over Fiona's questionable business practices?"

"Are you saying he might've come back and killed Fiona? That *is* a stretch. Nobody's ever been that loyal to me. Nobody."

Jeff stood, paced the floor. "Somebody did it. And, since it wasn't you, we have to look under every speck of dirt."

"Plenty of that in Fiona's shop," Lanny said.

Jeff wondered whether Lanny simply meant dirt, or if he meant *dirt*. "When did the others leave?"

"I was mostly watching Fiona with Tom and Sally. But when they paid her and started toward the door, the guy in the cap was pulling it closed behind him. The jewelry couple was halfway to the door by then, and Tom and Sally trailed them out."

"And, that left you and Fiona alone."

"Yeah, but I wasn't there more than a minute. What was the point? She just kept saying that she'd try to find some more majolica."

"Well, your fight was over that majolica, and you were buying one of the pieces for me. We don't know yet whether it was mine, yours, or both that's a lot more valuable—for some reason—than we first realized. But I, for one, am getting curiouser by the minute."

Lanny ran his hands over his face. "Fiona's murder might have nothing to do with the majolica."

"Then again, it might have everything to do with it." Jeff realized that, in less than twenty-four hours, he and Lanny had traded opinions. He wondered why the sudden switch. But what about him? Had the hunt for majolica clouded his reasoning?

"The surveillance tape should help determine who came in after you left." Jeff paused. "One more thing comes to mind: Did Fiona seem remorseful at all?"

"She acted . . . weird. She kept saying that more of the stuff would turn up. And, she said something like, 'There's things much better than majolica. You'll learn that soon enough.'"

"How'd that make you feel?"

"How do you think it made me feel? It was like I was being offered a consolation prize. It made me mad."

Mad enough to kill her? the prosecution would ask.

Jeff sighed.

Lanny stood, effectively ending the conversation.

Jeff followed suit, walked over and tapped on the door. "Try to get some rest. I'll be back in the morning, and we'll see about getting you out of here."

"You're the only one who might be able to."

As Jeff drove home, he mulled over everything Lanny had told him. He spent the evening committing to memory the details about the witnesses. It wasn't until he prepared for bed that he realized he had dropped the ball while questioning Lanny. He hadn't asked the right question. *Maybe you don't know* who *would want to cause you trouble, Lanny, but I think you know* why.

EIGHT

LANNY, MORE THAN anyone else, had encouraged Jeff to go
into antiques. Jeff hadn't thought about it at the time, but it
meant not only that Lanny lost his supplemental informant's income but also that he had one more competitor in
the growing ranks of those ferreting out loot.

Jeff had always held a romantic regard for antiques,
and, in spite of that, had done well for himself when he'd
turned his love for collectibles into a career. He believed
that his nostalgia for antiques actually helped him—like,
in the case of old Mr. Hoffman.

Because he'd been a detective, Jeff had always approached his picker business like a detective. He used his
investigative skills to track down particular antiques for
clients, to learn who had what, who wanted what, who
would pay what. His sources had been as diverse as Patsy

Cline and Madonna, and oftentimes played out by following the gossip trail.

This latest lead on a big score had come about after Blanche mentioned that her neighbor reported that a cousin down in Steilacoom said that Mr. Hoffman, who was one of the town's oldest citizens and who had lived a miserly life in a house that hadn't been painted since Jimi Hendrix was born, was going to have to stop eating five crullers with his pot of coffee every morning or his arteries would end up so clogged with farm butter that no amount of angioplasty would prevent a heart attack. And, of course, everyone knew that old Mr. Hoffman's house was packed to the rafters with French and German antiques.

Most pickers hovered when they heard about people like Hoffman. They watched the obits, waiting to swoop in and grab up stuff at the estate sale. They drove past, searching for telltale signs of activity, or lack of activity. And, they gossiped. Jeff, on the other hand, put his trained skills to work, found out what he could about the person, then paid him or her a visit. You couldn't appear greedy, or needy, or uncaring.

Take old Mr. Hoffman, for instance. Jeff had paid him a call when all his competitors acted as if they were afraid to enter the mysterious house while the old man was alive. Wasn't that better, though, than going in after all life had died out? Sure, Jeff loved stuff. And, yes, sometimes, he became obsessed with it. But he tried to never get so caught up in mateialism that he couldn't be decent to his fellow human being. Usually, he succeeded.

That wasn't to say that all pickers were that way. Many, like the four women he'd met down at Puyallup, were friends. They looked out for one another, even went so far as to give one another rides if a vehicle broke down, or a husband needed the van to haul his son's soccer team to practice while his wife camped out at a particularly promising estate sale. They'd been in Portland when the fight had broken out that Jeff had told Lanny about. One of the women had muttered, "Men," in a way that apparently said it all, because the other three had said in unison, "No kidding," before they all turned their attention back to the front door in anticipation of the sale.

When Jeff had entered the old German's home the month before, he'd done so under no pretenses. As he'd told Hoffman, health care costs were unbelievable and there was no reason he should have to raid his savings when the sale of a choice few items of furniture might forego cashing in his bonds.

Jeff recalled his surprise at the old man's appearance on that first—and, so far, only—visit to the mystery house. Although white-haired, with a deeply creviced face that resembled a batch of dough before kneading, Hoffman's ramrod-straight posture filled the door frame, leaving just enough room to slide a sheet of copy paper through sideways. "Yes?"

"Mr. Hoffman? I'm Jeff Talbot. Thanks for agreeing to see me."

"I figured it was you, but you can't be too careful. Come in." He shut the door. "Friend of mine once answered the door with 'Mr. Weeks, you're half an hour early.' Turned out it wasn't Mr. Weeks, and my friend got robbed. His own fault, really, telling the stranger who he expected him to be, instead of waiting to hear who he was."

Hoffman took off down a long corridor, waving Jeff along with him. "Perfect timing. The baklava is just ready to come out of the oven."

The home was dark, yet cloaked in a warm amber glow created by several vintage lamps. Their gentle radiance created a cozy feeling, welcome on the cold, rainy afternoon. The aromas of rich coffee and caramelized sugar grew stronger as they neared the back of the house. Jeff's stomach growled, reminding him that he hadn't taken time to eat anything since breakfast. Coffee carried you only so far.

"Good." Hoffman glanced over his shoulder at Jeff. "You're hungry."

Nothing wrong with the old man's hearing, thought Jeff. "I guess so, but I wouldn't want to impose." Oftentimes, he hated this part, felt like a preacher making weekly calls on his flock. You tolerated weak coffee, stale muffins, and idle gossip as you put in the requisite moments before getting down to business so you could move on to the next parishioner and repeat the motions. From the scents in this kitchen, though, he was in for a treat.

"Nonsense. I don't have many visitors, and I welcome any excuse to exercise my baking muscles. Now that I've shared my culinary secrets with the woman I sold the bakery to, she doesn't have much use for me being underfoot down there." He pulled a sheet of pastries from the oven— his fluid movements making him look downright youthful—and placed it on the range-top. "We'll give these a minute." Another beckoning wave, and they were off, retracing their steps toward the front of the home.

Hoffman led the way into a parlor where a crackling fire was reflected in a sterling tea service that had been set up on the coffee table. "Sit," he said as he poured coffee into the cups.

Jeff shed his trench coat.

"Let me take that," the old man said. "I'm forgetting my manners."

"Thanks." Jeff handed over the coat. "Really, I don't want to be any bother."

"Nonsense. Start on that coffee while I get the baklava. It'll chase out the chill."

Jeff did as he was instructed, and felt the angst of the last few days melt away with each sip of the rich, hot liquid.

He scanned the room. A seventeenth-century French desk flirted with him from the corner. He considered taking a closer look but Hoffman returned and broke the spell.

DEBORAH MORGAN

The old man placed another tray next to the silver one. This latest held an exquisitely patterned set of dessert china—Limoges, Jeff believed—laden with the glistening little pastry squares. Hoffman used silver tongs to serve the treats. Jeff detected only a slight tremor in the man's hand—not much for someone in his eighties.

Jeff took the plate offered him, and thanked his host.

"Don't wait on me," Hoffman said as he piled several delicacies onto his own plate.

Jeff took a bite. The warm, buttery pastry melted on his tongue, satisfied his senses, and invoked cozy childhood memories that smelled like cinnamon and chocolate and everything that was good in the world. If he lived near Hoffman's bakery, his cholesterol count wouldn't know what had hit it. He said, "Sir, these are phenomenal. My wife's a chef, so I get more than my share of amazing dishes, but . . . wow. Amazing."

"It's a pleasure feeding people who know how to enjoy food. Where does she work?"

"She works from home, does special catering gigs." Jeff slapped his stomach, and added, "I have to work out, or I'd weigh three hundred pounds."

"I'm surprised I don't. The years of eating rich foods are catching up with me, though, according to my doctor. Got news for him: I'm not changing." Hoffman sighed, settled back into his chair. His next words were faint. "He'll earn his keep, trying to keep my tick-tock ticking." He sank into the chair and closed his eyes.

Jeff imagined him sitting there night after night, reading, watching TV, working crossword puzzles—anything to pass the time.

Hoffman opened his eyes and swept his hand to take in the room. "I brought all this with me from the old country." His voice was strong again, as if some inner motor had been rewound. "Most of the French pieces were crafted by my grandfather, and the German pieces came from my father's family."

The workmanship on the furniture was perfection. They both knew why Jeff was there. Rather than tell the old man what he could get for the stuff, however, Jeff took the human approach. "You were close to your grandfather?"

"Yes, son, I was. He'd hoped I would follow in his foot-steps—he'd tried to teach my father the craft of cabinet-making, but it didn't take. When he saw that I was no good at it, that I'd rather be in the kitchen making strudel with my grandmother, he encouraged me to be a baker. I was a top pastry chef in Europe. That's how I saved the money to come to America and open my own bakery."

"You were fortunate. Too many parents don't recognize the gifts their children have. Instead, they push them to choose a career based on how much money it'll make. So, you hold on to these things because they're a connection to your family, your roots?"

"Truth be told, I've never questioned it. You seem sin-cere with *your* question, though, and it's something I've never been asked before."

"I am sincere," Jeff said. "I'm always curious as to why people collect."

"Collect? Oh, I'm not a collector, Mr. Talbot. I've just never considered selling anything. Of course, I didn't have children, so there's no one to pass them down to. I've won-dered whether, when I'm dead and gone, some distant rel-ative will come over here and try to claim all this."

"I suspect your grandfather would rather it served you." Jeff gradually got around to the mercenary side of things. "Isn't it better—as long as there's no one to pass this along to—that it help you live a long and comfortable life?"

"I've had the stuff for so long, I figure it makes me comfortable. Sort of like having another heartbeat in the house. Do you know what I mean?"

"Yes, I do. But isn't it better to see that your own heart can continue beating to enjoy your favorite pieces, than to quit on you because you tried to maintain *all* the pieces?"

From the expression on the man's face, Jeff knew that

Hoffman hadn't looked upon each piece as its own entity in years, probably since he'd first moved in and had worked sixteen-hour days at the popular bakery. It was clear: He'd never considered keeping only his favorites, and selling off the rest. Jeff continued, "If you did that, you could recapture the feeling you had about each piece, the feelings you had while you watched your grandfather bring them to life. They'd be new again, and refreshed memories go a long way toward renewing and invigorating the spirit."

"I'll tell you one thing," Hoffman said around a tiny cake he'd popped into his mouth, "you've got an approach different from everyone else. Oh," he added with a flap of his splotched hand, "no other antique dealers have come to the house—another thing I give you points for, son. It's not that I want them showing up, mind. But they act so blasted sneaky about what they're up to—like I don't have a brain just because I'm old. They go behind my back, talk to the gal who bought the bakery, quiz my doctor's receptionist. Thank God the HIPAA privacy laws are being enforced. If that receptionist were to tell them I broke a fingernail in their waiting room, I could have her canned. She wouldn't, but still . . . Anyway, the vultures act like I've got the damned plague, instead of a little plaque in my arteries."

Jeff knew when to keep quiet, let his suggestion kick in.

"Tell you what, Talbot," the old man continued. "I'm going to study every stick of furniture, see what triggers memories. If there are any pieces that don't, I'll call you."

Jeff had left Hoffman's home with no gut feeling whatsoever. His approach would either work or it wouldn't. The man would call, or not. That was the picking game, Talbot style.

⚘

Jeff hadn't thought about that first visit to Frenchie Hoffman's for over a week, and Lanny's comment had moved it to the front burner. Now, the need to generate income fought for mental real estate against trying to help Lanny, attempting to find majolica, locating Tom Walcher and Mustang Sally, then trying to coerce information from them. It might as well be fighting for space next to developing a cancer cure, for all the good it was doing him.

NINE

In JEFF'S WOODIE after Monday's arraignment, he said to Lanny, "I learned more about you in there than I have in the—what's it been?—seven or eight years I've known you."

Lanny gazed out his window. "What didn't you know?"

"Where you live, how old you are—you're a few years younger than I thought, by the way—that your legal name really is John Smith."

Lanny threw him a quizzical look. "You wrote it on a check. How'd you think I'd cash it if I couldn't prove it was my name?"

"I didn't mean it that way. Where'd the Lanny come from?"

"Just a nickname I picked up along the way. Why'd the judge release me on my own recognizance?"

"On *our* recognizance, I guess you'd say. I worked with

that judge several times back in the day; I assured him you weren't going anywhere." Jeff pointed out a pizza joint between James and Cherry. "How's that for lunch?"

"Sure. And, I won't."

"Won't what?"

"Go anywhere."

They made quick work of The GASP (garlic, artichoke, sun-dried tomatoes, and pesto pizza), then drove east toward Pioneer Square. After a stop at the bank so Lanny could withdraw the money Jeff had given him earlier to purchase the majolica, they made their way to Fiona's shop.

Jeff was surprised to find street parking in front of the place, and took advantage of it. In a moment, he and Lanny stood in front of Garden Gate Antiques, probably named for the antique wrought-iron gates bolted across the glass for security. The display window needed cleaning, and the old stained-glass window in the vintage shop door was partially boarded over. A remnant of yellow caution tape the size of a checkbook flapped between two of the boards.

"The last time I was in there," Jeff said, "her place was starting to look junked up. Kind of unusual for Pioneer Square nowadays."

"Yeah. Used to be, she'd have the best window display in the Square. But arthritis made it hard for her to get anything done the last couple of years." Lanny went to the window, cupped his hands around his eyes, and peered inside. "Too dark to tell if the globe's there."

Before gentrification took the area back to its glory days and made Pioneer Square the city's first historic district, the place was so unsavory that a few city officials proposed leveling it to make space for fresh, new office buildings and parking lots. Jeff never followed thinking that promoted destruction of history. At one time (likely during the sixties), the storefront brick had been painted a shade of raspberry that had long since weathered to a muddy mauve. Only the suggestion of a stenciled design remained, hinting at green vines and blue and yellow flowers.

"How'd Fiona land this prime piece of real estate?"

"She got a loan back when there were incentives to re-build this area. She was in her mid-twenties. Said she was too young to be scared. With a little money and a lot of guts, she told the banker she'd still be here peddling her wares while the bank fought off unwanted mergers and embezzling employees."

"With that kind of insight, she should've been running Boeing."

"She had a pretty good business sense."

Jeff popped his forehead with his palm. "I should've pulled around back. That's where your pickup is, right?"

"Should be, flat tire and all. The cops didn't ask if I had a vehicle, and I didn't volunteer the information."

"Didn't you have the keys on you?"

"Yeah, but when I told them where I live, they must've jumped to the conclusion that I didn't have wheels. Most people over there don't. The desk cop asked why I had all the keys, so I told him I collected them."

"Come to think of it, I'll bet the judge did the same thing when you told him you've had an apartment at the Morrison for the last few years."

"Yeah, we're all stereotyped. If they knew more of the background stories, they'd find more than a few people with better educations and credentials than their own ranks have. Thanks again, man, for helping me get outta there."

Jeff waved him off.

A woman came out of the shop next door. She was holding a pet carrier.

"Lanny?" she said as she approached the pair.

Lanny glanced at her. "Hi, Meredith."

"Should you be here?"

Lanny jerked his head toward Jeff. "As long as he knows where I am, I can be anywhere."

"Is he a cop?"

"I'm not a cop."

Lanny said, "Meredith owns Sufficient Grounds."

Jeff glanced at the storefront. Its display window held a wild yet artful array of mugs and cups, huge glass containers of roasted beans, and coffee carafes. A Halloween theme had been added with window clings of pumpkins and bats. Below them, a block-printed sign echoed the orange and black. It read, "October Special: For every cup of espresso sold, I'll give a schoolkid warts."

Jeff chuckled. "You should've put that sentiment in a letter to the editor."

"I did, right before the vote. They wouldn't run it, told me to send it to the *Salem Evening News*. So, I did. The AP picked it up, and my tourist traffic has doubled." She turned to Lanny. "I've got Dry Rot," she said, hoisting the carrier. She laughed then, and said to Jeff, "Fiona's cat. But he's freaking out Colette."

"Colette?" Jeff said.

"My poodle."

Lanny stooped, peered into the cage. "Tom told me you had him."

"Too bad cats can't talk," Meredith said. "He probably knows who killed Fiona."

"Believe me," Jeff said, "talking pets are a pain."

"Lanny, what's your friend smoking?"

"Nothing, Meredith. His wife just got three birds: two parrots and a crow. They all talk."

"I see."

Lanny indicated the container. "How'd you get the cat carrier?"

The woman set it on the sidewalk. "Same way I got the cat. I have a key to Fiona's shop."

Jeff instinctively glanced at the piece of yellow caution

tape, the boards over the door's window. "Do the cops know you have a key?"

She looked Jeff up and down. "No, and if you tell them, I'll call you a spiffed-up liar. Who'd you say you are?"

Lanny jumped in. "He's cool, Meredith. He's a picker, mostly for Blanche over by the piers."

"You'll get no argument from me, ma'am," Jeff said. "About the key. I think it's smart to keep it a secret."

"We have to take care of our own down here," she said.

"Got it," Jeff said. "Missus, uh . . . Meredith, did you notice anything unusual at Fiona's on Saturday?"

"You know, the cops asked me that very same question." She leaned toward Lanny. "If it walks like a duck . . ."

"Really Meredith, he's okay."

She studied Lanny's face intently. At last, she said, "I'll take your word for it, then. End of story."

"Thank you," Jeff said.

"Don't thank me. Thank Lanny."

"We came to get my pickup. I can take Dry Rot off your hands, if you want me to."

"Ha. Like your landlord's going to allow that."

"Tom's covering things today. I'll get him to help me."

"Suit yourself." She started to walk away.

"I can't take the carrier, too."

Meredith looked around. "Give me five minutes. I'll unlock Fiona's back entrance, if you promise to give me time to clear out. You can put the carrier inside."

"Appreciate it."

After she'd left, Lanny turned to Jeff. "I guess we're done. Thanks again for the help this morning."

"Wait." Jeff gazed down the sidewalk, watched the foot traffic. Those who weren't self-absorbed were absorbed in conversation with their companions. As they walked past, no one even seemed to notice that the shop was closed, the door's glass boarded over. He couldn't believe what he was thinking. If they were caught—or even seen—Lanny would be back in jail faster than a snake can strike. And, this time, Jeff would be right beside him.

He looked at Lanny. "What's that saying? When God closes a door . . . ?"

"He opens the back door?"

"Close enough."

"Are you sure you want to do this? I mean, you already stuck your neck out for me once today."

"We won't have another chance like this one."

"I'll take the alley, since I've got this." He waggled the pet carrier. The cat squalled.

Jeff nodded, walked toward the corner.

TEN

By THE TIME Jeff stepped inside the dim antiques shop, Lanny had freed Dry Rot from the carrier and poured a bowl of milk for him. Dry Rot shot a furtive glance Jeff's way, and positioned himself more solidly between human and bowl as he continued his lunch.

"You're the one with training," Lanny said. "What do we need to look for?"

Jeff had considered this as he'd walked around to the back. "Have you checked yet for the celestial globe?"

"Not yet."

"Do that, and make sure no one sees you through the window. I'll start back here, see if I can pick up anything from the paper trail that the detectives might have missed. In general, try to keep both your mind and your eyes open."

Lanny started toward the front.

Jeff held out no hope for ephemera. Investigators would've taken checkbook, register and credit card receipts, file folders, letters of provenance, the calendar, grocery lists . . . His list of lists could go on and on, a testament to the blight known as The Paperless Society. *The more to gather, the more to miss,* he thought as he opened desk drawers.

He came up empty. His nose started itching, and he pulled a tissue from the box on the desktop.

On the wall beside Fiona's desk was a row of white porcelain soap dishes holding an array of postage stamps, buttons, keys, thumbtacks, and spools of thread. Further investigation revealed no common denominator among the items: the thread didn't match the buttons, the stamps were a hodgepodge of everything from one-centers nearly a hundred years old to thirty-seven-centers printed last week. The same with the keys—some appeared to belong to cheap file cabinets while others were Victorian skeletons and gate keys.

Above the soap dishes was a cork bulletin board crammed with coupons, newspaper clippings (mostly comic strips and Kovel's antiques columns), a few old postcards, and quotes. Odd that those gathering evidence would pick clean the bones of the desk, yet leave all this on the corkboard. He read the quotes most prominently displayed:

"Women and cats will do as they please, and men and dogs should relax and get used to the idea."
—ROBERT A. HEINLEIN

"Thousands of years ago cats were worshipped as gods. Cats have never forgotten this."
—ANONYMOUS

"Time spent with cats is never wasted."
—COLETTE

"Right," Jeff said to no one in particular. "Tell that to Meredith's dog."

Lanny returned. "I've looked everywhere. The globe's gone. Maybe he came back and bought it."

"That might be all the more reason to find him. You'll need to let the authorities know about it, so they can check the surveillance tapes. Not much of a window between your last two visits here."

"I hope the tapes turn up something," Lanny said. "I finally talked them into letting me look through mug shots while I was in jail—nothing better to do. I saw a few guys that I've seen on the streets lately but—"

"Did you point them out to anyone?"

"And blow my cover as an informant? You're kidding, right?"

"I wasn't sure you were still in that line of work."

Lanny ignored the comment. "Nothing turned up in the mug files that'll help with this case. You find anything in the desk?"

"Nah, let's look up front some more."

Jeff surveyed the shop. "Are you sure they haven't found the murder weapon?"

"That's what they told me."

"I wonder how much time they invested going through all this stuff?"

"The murderer probably wasn't in here more than a minute or two." Lanny carefully lifted an Art Deco statuette, examined it, put it back down. "Do you think he brought the weapon with him?"

"Seems strange, carrying around something to hit a person in the back of the head with."

Jeff browsed, purveyed the stacks of dusty books, the tables crowded with tools, glassware, baskets of handkerchiefs, boxes of old sheet music. The surfaces of bureaus and sideboards were crowded with pottery and heaps of picture frames, and their drawers were opened slightly to reveal linen napkins, coils of faded ribbons, jumbles of tarnished silverware. Disney Pez dispensers leaned against a pair of Egyptian obelisks fine enough to grace the mantels of Buckingham Palace. Considering the popularity of Pez, Jeff couldn't be sure which collectible was more valuable. The obelisks won out for the moment as Jeff considered the possibility that they could be used as murder weapons.

Much of the merchandise wore a film of dust and print powder that revealed multiple fingerprints on everything. Jeff suspected that CSI gave up on the fruitless task, opting for one of their high-tech gizmos that would show whether an item held further evidence of foul play.

The junkiness put him in mind of a basement portion of Blanche's—she called it TLC, which meant the items needing tender loving care were there, at discount prices. His path crossed Lanny's, and he said, "I should've offered to take you by Blanche's on our way here."

"That's okay. I'll fill her in later."

They split up again, and Jeff made his way to the glass case that formed an *L* with a table holding an ancient cash register. In the case he found tray after tray of cuff links, rhinestone and marcasite jewelry, and a few Civil War uniform buttons.

A pair of bone cuff links with unusual carvings caught his eye. He stooped, tried to get a better view but couldn't. Lost in the moment, he rose to ask the proprietor for a closer look at the links. Then, he remembered himself, realized that he couldn't purchase anything. He glanced at Lanny to see if he had noticed, but the young picker was carefully weeding through hardware piled in an old wooden crate.

"Anything interesting?" Jeff asked as he stooped next to Lanny.

"Same old, same o—" He interrupted himself. "Look at that." He pointed out a faint rectangular pattern surrounded by residue on the soiled rug next to the demo box. It looked a little like the print powder, combined with mostly soot, ashes, and dirt. Jeff lifted the box. Underneath was a fine layer of the soot. Only, this rectangle had a shoeprint in the middle.

Jeff stood up, fought off a sneeze. "That's a big print."

"And, it hasn't been disturbed. Makes you wonder whether the cops even walked through this part of the shop, doesn't it?"

"I'd say they spent all their time searching for finger-prints, from the looks of the powder everywhere."

"They were looking for the wrong kind of print, then."

"First responders probably gathered up anything that might have served as a weapon, then left the rest to the de-tectives and CSI. They, in turn, gathered up anything that looked promising, with plans to return here if they came up with nothing but dust and dead ends."

"Do you think the killer was even out here, in the front of the shop?" Lanny glanced toward the street.

"Heck, he might've walked right through the front door. You said Fiona needed money. What if someone who looked like he had money showed up just before closing and charmed her into letting him browse? I've had it hap-pen—a shop owner giving me twenty minutes or so before shooing me out." Jeff looked again at the storefront, then at Lanny. "I think the killer waltzed through the front door, killed Fiona—for whatever reason—then, maybe, bailed out the back."

"Bad luck, you know. Not going out the same door you entered."

"Don't tell me you're superstitious."

Lanny raised his brows. "Why take chances?"

"You don't happen to know whether Fiona kept back-ups of anything, duplicates of sales receipts, stuff like that, do you?"

"If I do, does it incriminate me?"

Jeff looked at him. "Is that why you waited till I finally thought to ask?"

"It's a good reason."

"You know where her backup files are, don't you?"

No answer.

Jeff exhaled. "If there's evidence, it could vindicate you."

Lanny stared at him a moment. "Okay. Follow me."

He led the way to a small storage closet under the staircase that led to Fiona's upstairs apartment. "Fiona kept letters of provenance in a hidden filing system. That way, if anyone were to steal something that could be turned for a large profit, it was buyer beware."

"I should've thought of that sooner. More people are into documentation now."

Lanny opened the door.

A dozen mop and broom handles fell toward them and clattered to the floor.

Jeff jumped back. "Man, you might've warned me."

"Sorry. Good news, though. Probably means no one opened this. Most people would be inclined to prop the stuff against the door facings if they were putting them back. Fiona did it this way on purpose."

"Why?"

"Is your heart pounding?"

"You know damn well it is."

"That's why. And she'd know if anyone was messing around down here while she was upstairs."

"It would work," Jeff said. "Of course, a cop might've done the same thing, just to give the next person who opened it a jolt."

"I don't think it'll matter," Lanny said, scooting a couple of large, galvanized buckets fitted with mop-head ringers out of the way, then popping a fake wall panel out of the back of the closet.

"How long have you known about that?" Jeff asked.

"A couple of years now. She had me help her a few times on account of the arthritis."

The incriminate-vindicate dilemma struck Jeff again. On the one hand, the victim seemed to have trusted Lanny completely. On the other hand, investigators could have a field day with this.

Lanny must have sensed Jeff's concern. "I'm digging a deeper hole for myself, aren't I?"

Jeff moved a shoulder. "Let's see first if there's anything in the files that might help solve this."

Lanny reached inside and pulled a cord. Dim light stretched toward the corners of a box-shaped area of floor space about seven or eight feet square. Most of the floor was filled with stacks of lidded boxes that had originally held reams of printer paper. A few large grocery bags—the brown paper ones—and shopping bags from various department stores were crammed into the space atop the boxes.

From the front, Lanny pulled out an accordion file. "This is what she kept recent receipts and stuff in."

Dry Rot sidestepped Jeff and darted for the secret room, but Lanny scooped him up. "Oh, no you don't. The last thing we need is to try to get you out of all that junk."

Jeff sneezed. "I guess it's true what they say about curiosity killing the cat. He braved me to get to the closet."

Lanny doused the light and replaced the panel while he juggled feline and folder. Jeff put the buckets back and was juggling mop handles when he heard something up front. He glanced at Lanny, who was wide-eyed. He'd heard it, too.

Jeff jabbed air, pointing toward the back door.

Lanny bolted.

Jeff propped mops against the closet's inside wall—the trap no longer mattered—and, silently closing the closet door, he turned toward the back of the shop. There was no sign of Lanny. *Maybe,* Jeff thought as he shot toward the back door, *there's something to that superstition, after all.* As he pulled the door shut behind him, Jeff stole a glance at the front entrance. Detective Chris Fleming stepped over the threshold, followed by a uniformed cop.

ELEVEN

*J*EFF MADE A beeline for next door, grateful that Meredith's back entrance was marked as such for customers. He took a deep breath, then worked his way up front, ordered a cup of black coffee, and sat at one of the tiny tables. He gulped the hot coffee under the wary eye of the proprietor, and recalled what he knew about the young detective he'd just seen entering Fiona's shop.

There was no mistaking the very tall and very slender Chris Fleming. He'd made a name for himself in Seattle after solving the Four on the Floor murder case the previous year, and Jeff had gotten to know him during that time. Jeff's old partner, Gordy Easthope, had stayed at the Talbot home while working to bust the car theft ring tied to that case, and Fleming had practically lived there, too, working with Gordy.

The fact that Fleming was the detective on the Brock

murder case had probably been in the Sunday papers, and since the Talbots' Sunday household routine—newspaper, brunch, general leisure—had been disrupted with company, work, and a jail visit, Jeff had missed it.

Jeff managed to consume most of the cup of coffee before Fleming peered through the front glass of the shop, spotted him, and stepped inside. Jeff braced himself as Fleming approached.

"Jeff," Meredith said, slapping him on the back and startling the hell out of him, "is that second cup any better than the first?"

He recovered quickly. "Yes, Meredith, thanks. It's stronger than the first blend. The older I get, the stronger I drink it."

"No problem." She looked to Fleming. "May I help you?"

"Nothing for me, thanks." He sat across from Jeff without an invitation.

"Interesting," he began, "finding you here, leisurely"—he tilted his head, studied Jeff's face, chest, hands—"enjoying a cup of coffee next door to a crime scene."

Jeff was grateful that his regular workouts had paid off: his chest wasn't heaving, his heart wasn't beating rapidly, his face didn't feel flushed from the adrenaline or the physical strains of getting out of Fiona's shop in such a hurry.

"You know I'm a java junkie. You also know you can't arrest me for it."

"Can't miss that car of yours."

Poker face in place, Jeff thought. He winced. "Didn't I feed the meter?"

Fleming tilted his head to the right, toward the antiques shop. "When's the last time you were in there?"

"I work more with Blanche Appleby's shop over by the piers. All Things Old." Jeff drank. "Have you found the murder weapon yet?"

Fleming studied him for a long time. "No. You got any ideas what it might've been?"

Jeff didn't. "Give me something to go on."

"How much did your friend tell you?"

Jeff filtered information as he answered the detective, gave a thumbnail sketch of what Lanny had reported, then added, "He said that there wasn't much blood, and that it was a stack of five cut marks at the base of her skull. He thought it looked like a musical staff."

"I don't care what he thought it looked like. Did he put it there?"

"My opinion? No."

"Let's shelve that for now. Any idea *what* put them there?"

"I've been considering that myself. Not many things can make a set of lines. Maybe something used repeatedly?"

"Not according to the ME. One blow. She died instantly."

"Doesn't sound like an amateur, does it?"

"You're not suggesting a professional killer, are you?"

"No." Jeff gave this some thought. "Maybe. Who knows? I meant, what if the killer's someone with medical training, someone who checked for a pulse after that one blow, and knew beyond any doubt that she was dead?"

"That's a point. Still, one blow with *what?*"

"Maybe you need to look more closely at all that junk. Did the cops give you any possible murder weapons when you arrived on the scene?"

"Yeah," Fleming said, removing a small notepad from his breast pocket, "but the ME ruled out all of them. A decorative piece from an andiron, some tools they found in a box next to the victim's desk—rasp, level, screwdrivers, stuff like that. Also, a candlestick, a mantel clock, a couple of telescopes, a metal arrow—off a weathervane, I'm guessing." Fleming looked up from the list. "Do you know how many collectibles can be used as weapons?"

"All of them?" Jeff ventured.

Fleming grunted. "Probably."

"Question: When the cops arrived on the scene, was the front door locked or unlocked?"

"Unlocked. Your buddy was sitting across from the victim. Typically, it freaks people out to be in the room with a dead person. When asked why he was sitting there, he said he didn't want to leave her alone."

Jeff wondered whether Lanny's time alone—before the cops and paramedics arrived—had been enough time to do anything, or to check anything. Likely not, or he could have gotten to the accordion file that he'd taken today from the closet. A bell went *ding!* inside his head so audibly that he glanced at Fleming to see whether he'd heard it, too. But the detective was busy skimming his notes.

Lanny had just fled with the file. Jeff would've found it much more comforting to have gone over its contents *with* Lanny—not after the young picker had already had a go at it.

Jeff needed to find Lanny, and the sooner the better. It'd be a chore, shaking loose from Fleming, making sure he wasn't tailed while he went over to Lanny's apartment building. Then, add the chore of finding out which apartment was Lanny's. Likely, the tenants were either close-knit and didn't give squat to outsiders, or they were loners who didn't give squat to anybody. The only thing Jeff knew for a fact: Lanny knew more than he was letting on.

He needed to move. At the same time, he didn't want to keep the latest clue from the authorities and risk having it inadvertently destroyed. "Fleming, your team might've missed a clue when they were there earlier. There's an undisturbed footprint—*shoe*print, I should say—over by a player piano against the south wall."

"How do you know about a shoeprint in a sealed-off crime scene?"

"I'm trying to help you here."

"You're trying to help that picker friend of yours."

"That's a bonus."

"Answer my question."

Jeff stared at him evenly. "Call it ESP."

"Talbot." Fleming leaned back, rubbed his eyes. "You know I need better than that."

"You need to solve a murder. You need to know that the shoeprint probably doesn't belong to one of the dozen or so cops that were likely wandering around that junked-up shop, not having a clue where to start searching for a clue—let alone a murder weapon."

"Okay, okay. If it *does* belong to one of my officers, I'll . . ." He let it drop.

"Anyone over there now?"

"Yeah, I left Holcomb over there to—" Fleming jumped up, shot toward the door. He turned. "Aren't you coming, Talbot?"

～～～

Holcomb was a uniformed officer under thirty, with a stocky build, a blond crewcut, and a plump, ruddy face. He was hovering over the shoeprint by the box. He glanced up when the pair entered, then quickly returned his gaze to the print, as if he were afraid it would walk off. "Detective, you'll want to see this. It doesn't make any sense."

Fleming squatted on his haunches and studied the print. "Why do you say that?"

"Because, if it had been here the day of the murder, wouldn't someone have pointed it out to forensics so they could photograph it and cast it?"

"You'd think so, wouldn't you?" said Fleming, irritation evident in his tone. He stood.

Since Fleming didn't ask the obvious question, Jeff did. "How do you know it hasn't been photographed?"

Holcomb smiled. "My girlfriend works CSI. She showed me the photos."

Fleming punched numbers on the cell phone he'd retrieved from its clip on his belt and, with clenched jaw, said, "Alexis, I'm at the Brock murder scene. Send forensics back over here."

TWELVE

FLEMING DISMISSED JEFF before forensics showed up, which Jeff viewed as both a blessing and a curse. Fortunately, Fleming was preoccupied enough with the missed shoeprint that he probably wouldn't think to put a detail on Jeff. Of course, now Jeff wouldn't be privy to any new discoveries.

He needed to hook up with Lanny, and the Morrison was within walking distance, but leaving the woodie parked where it was would only raise more suspicion with Fleming. Jeff shouldn't have driven it at all that day but, since he had, he needed to remove it from Fleming's radar as much as possible. He rolled away from the curb and drove the few blocks. After stowing the car in a parking garage, he set out walking.

The more time Jeff spent with Lanny, the more he liked him. It'd been strange at first, engaging in normal dialogue, as opposed to the covert exchanges of information they'd conducted in the past. At the same time, he wondered about Lanny's past. He had an education, he had manners. That much was evident, if one looked beyond the cover of the tattered book. He also had a different attitude toward his so-called lot in life from what Jeff had expected. Lanny seemed comfortable with his life, not downtrodden. He wasn't someone who knocked The Establishment. Jeff found himself wondering what had brought Lanny to this place, what his background was. But he'd try not to pry, except about things that might have a direct bearing on the case.

The Morrison sat just off Skid Row, a term that originated in the Emerald City as Skid Road when pioneers dragged logs down the steep incline of Yesler Way to the waterfront to be milled. The structure, eight stories built of, one might say, Yukon gold brick, was once a luxury hotel that housed the exclusive Arctic Club: a group of men who'd returned from the Yukon glittering with gold dust and tales of adventure.

It had started out as the Arctic in the early nineteen hundreds, and was outgrown in half a decade, at which time the members of the club commissioned the design of their new home a couple of blocks north.

The original building became the Morrison, and was now a neglected structure paired with a neglected society: the homeless.

As a boy, Jeff had learned the history of the Alaska Gold Rush and the ornate buildings erected in Seattle as a result of the fortunes made. Whether those lessons had come from the aunt who had raised him or from his schoolteachers, he no longer remembered. But he remembered the fascinating stories, and how he and Sam Carver would play make-believe, digging for gold in their own backyards. (Sam was the one with the vivid imagination, and had always instigated their escapades.) These experiences, perhaps, had led to Jeff's love of finding treasure, for during those gold digs he'd unearthed old keys and coins, a watch fob, and even a garnet ring that was said to have belonged to his great-grandmother. His aunt Primrose had cautioned him not to reveal his discovery to his grandfather, but to hold on to it as a gift for his own wife when he married. The ring was still one of Sheila's most prized treasures.

Jeff wasn't sure where to start searching for Lanny, so he stepped inside the ground level office of the Downtown Emergency Service Center. He'd read that the DESC was overseeing a major rehabilitation, and the current scene was like a hospital emergency room on a Saturday night.

When he'd finally reached the head of the line, he said, "I need to see someone who lives in the building."

"Check in on the second floor." The busy clerk didn't look up.

That was it? He'd waited twenty minutes, only to learn that he was at the wrong check-in point. He made his way to the second-floor desk, where the situation wasn't much different. A tall, muscular man with black hair and a clean-shaven face directed traffic, doled out over-the-counter medicines, tallied transients pouring out of the rain and into the building, provided assurance, checked ID cards, passed out coffee, signed people up for mats, calmed a self-proclaimed battered woman with two children in tow, and instructed a half-starved man to go to the Boomtown Café on the street level for a charitable meal.

Jeff's question felt trivial among it all. Nonetheless, he needed to hook back up with Lanny. "I need to see John Smith, please."

Someone behind him grunted. "Tom'll need more than that."

"You're Tom? Tom Walcher?"

"That's right," the man said as he eyeballed two more ID cards and nodded the people through. "Are you with DESC?"

"No, I'm a friend of Lanny's. He told me about you, how you helped Mustang Sally."

Walcher stared at Jeff for a moment, then yelled after one of the guys he'd ID'd. "Bill, tell Lanny he's got a visitor, would you?"

"Sure thing."

"Thanks."

"If he doesn't come down, we'll try again. Bill might not remember once he gets up there."

Unsure what to make of that, Jeff nodded once and made his way to the nearest wall and put his back against it. He watched the goings-on, and, the longer he stood there, the more he understood: The Morrison was home to those recovering from the busted hands that life had dealt them—drugs, alcohol, abuse, poverty. The guy called Bill might or might not remember whether he'd eaten today, let alone the favor Tom had asked him to do.

Jeff watched him disappear into the elevator cage, then 5 lit up above the doors. Was that Lanny's floor, or had Bill forgotten?

Jeff waited fifteen minutes before he tried again. "Walcher?" he said after the man had processed more incoming, sorted more outgoing, doled out supplies, and answered a phone that seemed to never stop ringing. "Is your job like this every day?"

"Like what?"

"Like . . . intense?"

"Pretty much."

"Listen, uh . . ."

"Lanny. Right." Walcher glanced at the wall clock. "Shift change in ten. If you can hang on, I'll go up and check on him myself when my replacement shows."

"Thanks."

It happened according to Walcher's promise. The only problem was that upon his return, the employee stepped from the descended elevator alone. "Sorry, man. He's not in. Want I should give him a message?"

"Yeah, I suppose. Just tell him that Jeff Talbot needs to talk to him, the sooner the better."

"Will do." Walcher nodded, shuffled wearily toward the exit.

As Jeff walked back to his car, he realized that the trip up to the fifth floor was above and beyond for someone whose job was more like a circus juggling act than anything else.

❦

Back home, Jeff gave Sheila a thumbnail sketch of his day. He told it in no particular order, starting with Lanny's release and ending with how Fleming had almost caught the two of them in Fiona's off-limits shop.

Sheila waved him off. "You would've found a way out of it. Besides, Chris is one of the fairest people I know."

"Huh?"

"Remember, his mother and I are friends."

Jeff hadn't remembered. Since Sheila never left the house, and since most of her friends were via online chat rooms and message boards, they didn't seem three-dimensional to him. He knew better than to tell *her* that.

"Would you cover the phone for about an hour?" Sheila asked. "I have to finish packing up auction sales for a pickup first thing in the morning, and Greer's out running errands."

"Sure. I'll catch up on some accounting."

After she went upstairs, he poured a large mug of coffee and took it with him to the library.

An hour later, Jeff was chasing down an elusive balance in his ledger when the phone rang. After the third bell, he remembered that he was in charge of the thing. He grabbed it just ahead of the answering machine.

After pleasantries, the voice on the other end said, "I'm confirming Sheila's doctor's visit for tomorrow morning."

"She mentioned it last night," Jeff said, "but I'll let her know you called."

After he'd hung up, Jeff jotted, "Dr Jen. Tue. 10a." on the message pad, and returned to his bookkeeping.

He surfaced half an hour later when he heard Sheila on the stairs at the back of the house. He grabbed his mug and the message, and went to the kitchen for more coffee.

"Thanks, hon," she said as he handed her the note.

"No problem." He dumped the cold coffee into the sink.

"Actually," Sheila said, "it's Jenn with two *n*s."

He filled the mug with hot coffee. "What difference does it make?"

She grabbed a notepad and pen from beside the kitchen phone, and jotted something. "Here, hon, you have a message."

He took the note. It read: "Thanks, Jef."

"Okay, okay, I get your point." He swigged coffee. "I should be gone all day tomorrow, anyway."

"Jeff," she said, wrapping her arms around his waist, "you don't have to make yourself scarce during my appointments. I really don't mind."

He kissed her cheek. "Still, I like to give you your space." He'd made it a habit to stop by the house most days that he was working locally, and felt it helped balance the times he'd been traveling farther outside home base in search of antiques. But he'd be busy, trying to get a lot done before winter. "I've got a lead on some stuff down near Longview, so I'm planning an early start."

"Of course," he continued, "that's *after* I find Lanny."

THIRTEEN

◦═══◦

*H*E TRIED TO find Lanny again on Tuesday.

Or, at least, it started out that way. Jeff left the house early, deducing that if he hit the Morrison in the morning instead of the afternoon, he might have better luck. He'd touch base with Lanny, find out what was in the files from Fiona's secret closet, and still have time to make Longview by early afternoon.

He finally found parking a scant three blocks away, and was almost to the hotel's entrance when he spotted the woman who had to be Mustang Sally.

She was over six feet, and wore a camel coat. Wrapped around her neck was what he recognized as the camel, red, white, and black plaid of a Burberry scarf—only dingier. She saw him, too, did an about-face slicker than a marching band, and all but jogged down the sidewalk.

Jeff followed.

She covertly glanced over her shoulder, and he quickly feigned disinterest. This happened three or four times before she clearly sensed that she was being tailed. She took off at a full run, dodging and weaving through pedestrian traffic, and turned right at the corner.

When she broke into a run, Jeff did the same, ignoring the mental red flag that told him she could have him arrested.

It didn't matter. When he rounded the corner, she was gone. He walked the block, alternately glancing into store windows and checking the sidewalk ahead of him, but there was no sign of the young woman.

He'd lost her.

She's good, I'll give her that, he thought. She'd vanished so abruptly, so completely, that he actually wondered if she had stepped sideways into some alternate existence. Maybe Lanny was there, too, in that secret place that enveloped those fleeing from threat. They might be strolling along together at that very moment, the sun on their faces, no threat of hunger or danger, no need to look over their shoulders, no need to dodge pursuers like Jeff who seemed to have nothing but questions for people who had few answers.

An alternate universe. It crossed his mind that others might ponder this, too; might come to that conclusion as a means of coping when a loved one disappeared. Did Lanny and Sally, and others like them, have people somewhere who loved them, missed them, wondered every day, every moment, whether the missing were in danger, whether they were still alive, or whether they'd hopefully found this alternate existence in which to escape, to survive?

How had he made it as an agent? Had people on the streets gotten smarter? Had his own street sense gone to seed? And, where was the simple life he'd planned for by leaving behind this cat-and-mouse game?

He doubled back to the Morrison, and played a rerun of

Monday's Find Lanny Show. His consolation prize was a weak cup of coffee from Walcher.

They left the building together. Walcher said, "You coming back this afternoon?"

"Nah," Jeff said, "I'll see you tomorrow."

"I know I'll be here." Walcher stepped out into the rain.

Jeff pulled the hood of his jacket over his head, and walked in the opposite direction.

He was starting to get the picture. The homeless community, along with those either connected to them or a scant thread away from being them, was a tight-knit community, a subculture, protective when outsiders tried to break down the wall. If Jeff had to guess, he'd say that none who knew Lanny believed him capable of murder, yet would admit that any one of them could—and would—kill if they had to. It all hinged on survival, and the streets had taught them nothing if not that.

He contemplated whether he'd stuck his neck out one too many times while trying to help. What if he'd misjudged Lanny's innocence—and his honesty?

It seemed dark and he checked his watch, then looked around, tried to get his bearings. Must've been the rain. It was a dark rain, and a dark, dead-end day.

He had the eerie feeling that someone was watching him. He twisted, saw nothing suspicious behind him. He turned back and pushed the hood from his head, choosing vision over the rain buffer. That's when he saw the eye. He stopped, and faced it.

From across the street, it seemed to watch him. The neon lid fluttered, creating the illusion that it had blinked. In an arc over the lid were the words PRIVATE EYE. Why had he never noticed it before? The address on the street-level door read 77 SOUTH MAIN. It put Jeff in mind of 77 Sunset Strip, and he wondered whether it was a coincidence. He stared back for a long time.

By the time he reached his car, he was drenched. It was too late for the trip south, and he was tired besides. He longed for a quiet evening with a warm fire and hot coffee and surroundings that had nothing to do with antiques or Halloween or murder.

There's no place like home, he thought, rolling north.

❦

Wearily, he climbed the back staircase, shucked the wet clothes, and showered quick and hot before climbing into well-worn cords and a long-sleeved T-shirt.

Much better, he thought as he walked from his dressing room. He called Sheila's name, got no answer, and was on the landing when Sheila's voice echoed from the first floor. "Somebody help!" she cried.

He shot down the stairs. "Where are you?"

"The conservatory! Hurry, Jeff!"

He ran into the room, found Sheila standing in front of Morty's cage with her fists pressed to her mouth. "Oh, Jeff, he's dead, isn't he? Look at him."

Jeff sighed in relief that Sheila was okay and he wrapped his arms around her. He didn't know much about birds but the brightly colored parrot did, indeed, appear to be dead. "Hon, I . . . I don't know what to say."

The bird's head turned then, and its body sprang to life. It hopped up onto its perch and said, "Play dead, Morty, play dead."

Sheila walloped the side of the cage. Morty flapped and squawked and deposited a gift for her on the *Seattle Times.*

"Don't you ever scare me like that again, you little ingrate, or I'll make you into roast squab."

The bird either squawked again or tried to repeat "squab," Jeff wasn't sure which. He stifled a laugh. "Welcome to motherhood, hon."

"Yeah, well." She straightened herself, shot a warning look at the bird, then went back to her chair. "I'm not sure I'm cut out for motherhood. Not this kind, anyway."

He hated to admit it but he hoped she'd tire of the birds and find new homes for them. He started to voice this but, remembering the warning Morty had gotten, decided to keep his bill shut.

She didn't seem to notice. "I thought you might be home soon, so I made coffee, too. Do you have time to join me?"

"Sure." Jeff sat opposite her, warmed her tea before pouring coffee for himself, then grabbed a snickerdoodle. "Where's Greer?"

"I gave him the afternoon off. He and Robbie have tickets to *Mourning Becomes Electra*. They're going to dinner before curtain."

"Good. I could use a quiet evening."

"Did you find Lanny today?"

"Nope." Jeff filled her in on the almost-meeting with Mustang Sally. He didn't tell her about his bizarre thoughts regarding an alternate universe, or the stare-down with the glass eye. The last thing he needed was for her to find a reason for him to talk to her counselor. "I might end up staking out the Morrison."

"You'd better do it before Chris decides he wants to talk to Lanny and comes to you when he can't find him."

"Chris? Oh, right. Fleming. That's all I need, the courts wanting Lanny and I'm the one who stuck my neck out for him."

"You don't think he's involved in anything, do you?"

"The murder? No. But something's going on, and I need to find out what it is."

A buzzer sounded from the kitchen. Sheila hopped up. "Are you going to find out tonight?"

Jeff grabbed his cup and trailed after her. "Probably not."

She pulled a glass loaf pan from the oven and set it on a wire rack to cool. "Relax, then, okay?"

"Easier said than done." He finished the snickerdoodle,

rummaged in the Shawnee cookie jar for another one. "Did Lee Dunbar call back yet?"

"She did. I'm sorry I didn't tell you when you first got here."

"What'd she say?"

"She's interested in several pieces from the Native American collection for an auction. I E-mailed more detailed photos to her."

"What about the jack-o'-lanterns?"

"She wants to buy them herself. I put a copy of her offer on your desk."

Jeff started toward the library but Sheila stopped him. "Can't you mess with it later? Lee was on her way out of the office, anyway."

"I suppose. Sorry. I'm just keyed up."

"Look, I've made a nice dinner, we'll watch a movie." She nuzzled his neck. "I have a bottle of wine chilling, something new I've been wanting to try. I think you should start on it, instead of more caffeine."

He shrugged. "Might as well see if it'll help."

"I hope it does. You haven't smiled since you got home."

"Sheila, I'm sorry. It's just that—"

She placed a finger over his lips. "Just give me one uninterrupted evening, and I'll relieve your stress."

She sidled up next to him. Jeff kissed her. He would try to play along. It wasn't going to be easy, pushing his suspicions about the murder case against Lanny to the back of his mind. He recognized how his mind worked, how he sank his teeth into a problem like a canine grip on a pants leg. It was like the stories he'd been told as a kid—how if a turtle got hold of you, it wouldn't let go till it thundered; or how an injured snake wouldn't die till sundown. Jeff's teeth had hold of this case. Sheila had thought that his obsession with a problem would magically stop with his retirement. So did he, for that matter. *Tell that to your senses,* Jeff thought as he allowed his wife to lead him upstairs.

Late that night, the calming effects of an evening with his wife were jostled.

Detective Fleming apologized for the late call after Jeff answered the phone.

"How's the case going, Detective?"

"Not like I'd hoped. I thought this one would be a cinch, after we learned about all the people who were present when Smith fought with the vic."

"So, you haven't found the murder weapon?"

"Not yet, we haven't."

"What about surveillance tapes?"

"I've gone through what we have but Murphy's Law has us in its grips. It looks like the vic took the cassette out after the fight with Lanny. Maybe she planned to file it away as evidence. She must've gotten distracted, or she didn't have any new tapes on hand, because there wasn't one in the equipment when her place was searched after her murder."

"What about that shoeprint?"

It took Fleming a beat to answer. "We've got a rookie cop who wears a size fourteen. He was coming up with murder weapon possibilities. He knocked over an urn, then stepped in the ashes that spilled from it. Worried that he'd sullied a crime scene, he set the crate over it. About the same time he saw that *that* wasn't going to work—the tell-tale rectangle it left—it dawned on him what kind of ashes they were. Now, he's so spooked, he's trying to switch shifts so he won't have to work patrol Halloween night."

"Hasn't he ever heard those three little words, 'extra patrol units'?"

"He will."

Jeff chuckled. "I don't envy you your job, Fleming."

"Yeah, well, back to the people I'm not employing. I can't get enough out of Tom Walcher to fill a Tylenol capsule, I can't get anything useful out of the office couple, I can't get anything *at all* on the guy who was near the front door, and I can't find the woman they call Mustang Sally."

"Can't find her? I saw her earlier today." The words escaped his mouth before his brain had properly filtered them. Regret kicked in.

"You saw her, as in 'Oh, I saw her walking down the opposite side of the street,' or, as in, 'I took her to lunch, learned her life story, and got her version of Saturday's incident, to boot?'"

Uh-oh. Best to spit it all out at once. "I saw her walking down the street, and I followed her with the intent of finding out the rest of that stuff you said. Only she spotted me and took off. I lost her."

"You lost her."

Jeff didn't have to see the detective's face to know that he'd turned red with anger. The detective blew out a long stream of air. Jeff pictured the spout on a pressure cooker. He waited.

"Talbot." Another sigh.

"Admit it, Detective. You would've done the same thing. I'll tell you this, though: You'd better find one long-legged gumshoe to keep up with her. She's like a gazelle."

"Have you forgotten who you're talking to?"

"Oh, right." Jeff envisioned Fleming and Mustang Sally standing back to back. Put her in two-inch heels and stretch a level over their heads and the bubble would be dead center.

"I suppose," Fleming said, exhaling once more, "I'll head over to the Morrison tomorrow, take another crack at Smith."

Tilt. He imagined trading the last six hours with Sheila for a tin tray and a cold cot, simply because he himself hadn't been able to find Lanny even though he was supposed to know his whereabouts. He might come clean on a lot of things, but he wasn't stupid. "Well, good luck with that, Detective."

FOURTEEN

THE GAME CONTINUED, only Jeff wasn't having any fun playing. He would show up at Tom Walcher's post, and Walcher would stop some Tom, Dick, or Harry (or the ubiquitous Bill), and ask him to let Lanny know that "that guy" was back to see him. Then nothing would ever come of it.

Now, it was Friday. *Friday.* He walked toward the Morrison, just as he had every day that week. Five days in a row, he'd reported here, and if he worked in one of the downtown office buildings, he'd be thinking about payday. *Thank God it's Friday.* The day before, he'd helped Tom with several large boxes—a shipment that Tom said held much-needed blankets for the winter. If he helped today, would that mean he was Tom's Gal Friday? *Friday.* He thought, *Lanny, I'm not doing this tomorrow.*

Jeff walked through the door and said, "Hey, Tom."

"Hey, Talbot."

"You work tomorrow, Tom?" he said as he leaned against the wall that had become his regular post.

"Yeah. You?"

"Depends, I guess."

Jeff debated going door-to-door, wondered how far he'd get before somebody suspected he was the eviction police and a red alert swept through the building like fire.

"As you know, I've been here every day this week. I'm losing patience. Lanny has no reason to ditch me, and I have to wonder if he's okay."

"He's okay." Tom sliced open a corrugated box, looked inside, then slid it into the room behind the counter. "I saw him last night."

"Yeah?" Jeff straightened. "Did you tell him I'm looking for him?"

Walcher lifted his gaze from the stack of mail he was sorting. "It came up. He told me he's been real busy."

Jeff stepped aside for a group of workers wearing tool belts and hauling in table saws, sawhorses, and slabs of one-by-twelves. To Walcher, he said, "This place will look great when they're finished."

"The original architecture is what's great. It's good to see that they're preserving as much of it as they can. This was the Arctic, originally, not the one over on Cherry where they give the tours. Cost half a mil to build and furnish this one, and that was nearly a hundred years ago."

Jeff wished he'd known earlier that this was the way to get the guy to talk. Of course, the lull in Walcher's chores was rare. "It sounds like you're into architecture."

Walcher said, "It's always been an interest of mine. Probably started with Tinkertoys when I was a kid."

The man called Bill entered the building and, without any prompting, offered to give Lanny the message.

A young woman with a baby riding on her hip walked up to Walcher's post and whispered something. He nodded and stepped through the opening to the small room behind the counter. When he did, someone else slid inside and tried to sneak past.

"Hey!" Tom said, bolting from the storeroom. He slapped a small, pink box on the counter as he wheeled around and took off after the guy. The woman scooped up the box and shoved it into her coat pocket before scooting down the corridor.

Jeff moved toward the hall, watched for Tom. No sign of him. Jeff paced, waited, listened. A door slammed, then another, farther away. Their sounds vibrated, echoed, till the last traces reached Jeff, finally, as a faint breath. Then, nothing.

He started past the elevator, but stopped directly in front of the doors. He looked down the hallway again. Nothing. The elevator doors opened. Jeff turned his head toward the cage. It was empty. And, as the doors began to close, he made a snap decision. One move sideways, and he was out of sight.

On the fifth floor, he glanced both ways, saw Bill pivoting from an apartment door halfway down the hall, next to a wall sconce. Jeff mentally bookmarked it.

Bill sidestepped stacks of two-by-fours as he walked to the end of the corridor and disappeared through a door. Had the guy been telling Lanny every time, Jeff wondered, or was this the first time he'd caught Lanny at home?

The corridor was a study in inconsistency, flophouse meets showpiece. Lingering odors of old grease, stale cigarettes, and something like sweat brought about from battling off defeat struggled against the bouquet of new-sawn lumber and fresh paint.

A couple of carpenters wearing goggles and white masks, their clothes coated in chalky dust, scraped paint from baseboards and moldings. Jeff batted dust motes as he made his way down the hall, wondering if the only lead poisoning he *wasn't* being exposed to was that used in the old pottery glazes.

When he reached the door that Bill had first stopped at, he raised his fist to knock as Lanny swung open the door.

"I was on my way down to get you."

"Since when? I've been down there for five days."

"Sorry about that. I've been gone a lot, doing a little investigating on my own."

Jeff said, "You left Seattle? After the judge let—"

"No, I didn't leave, much as I would've liked to. Give me some credit, would you? You vouched for me, and I told you I wouldn't leave. End of story."

They stared at each other.

"Did you turn up anything useful?" Jeff said.

Lanny stuck his head out the door and glanced toward the carpenters, then resumed his stance.

Jeff waited, finally said, "You want to do this out here, or can I come in?"

"Oh, sorry. I'm not used to company." Lanny stepped aside, and Jeff entered.

The apartment, which wasn't even large enough to be called a studio, was clean and orderly. It was sparsely furnished, containing a couch and a chair (mismatched), an olive drab four-drawer file cabinet (battle-scarred as if it had fought in World War II), a much smaller version of Sheila's old, oak teacher's desk, and, under the room's only window, a tiny Formica-and-chrome table with two matching chairs.

"Where do you sleep?"

"On the couch." Lanny tapped a small wall plaque, then walked to the kitchen counter. "You want coffee?"

"Sure." Jeff read the plaque's sentiment: "If you have a rug on your floor, you have too much." *Thought-provoking.* He said, "If the city sees how nice this place looks, they're likely to halt the renovation."

"It's just paint. I found several gallons at a garage sale last year. You can thin it with water and stretch it quite a bit without losing too much quality. I painted a few of the apartments, the ones where women stay, and a few for the old guys who can't do much for themselves anymore.

"That's part of why they haven't made me leave," Lanny continued. "Plus, I locate stuff like chairs, beds, utensils, anything that'll help make the rooms livable. Have a seat."

Jeff started for the couch but Dry Rot sprang out from under the desk, leaped onto the sofa, and stretched out as if to claim the length of it as his domain. Jeff took the chair.

Lanny handed him a mug (brown Frankoma from the seventies with a two-tone drip glaze), and Jeff noticed for the first time that Lanny's nails were impeccably clean, an oxymoron with the tattered, fingerless gloves he wore.

"I figured you'd track me down eventually," Lanny said, picking up the cat and seating himself on the couch, "so I put on a fresh pot every day when I got back here."

"That's a lot of late-night coffee." Jeff drank. "Good coffee, to boot. What made you think I'd find you?"

"You were a good agent. I'd have to rethink a lot of opinions about you if you couldn't find me in an eight-story building."

"I meant, what made you think I'd come looking for you?"

"You're bound to be curious about that folder we took from Fiona's closet. Truth is, I thought you'd catch up with me before now. I told Tom to expect you."

"Yeah? Why didn't he just send me up?"

"I really have been out most of the time. Tom's more protective than most, though, which is good—makes a lot of the people who live here feel safe for the first time in a long time. If ever."

Jeff settled back in the chair, crossed an ankle over a knee. "That makes a difference. I barely got out the back door of Fiona's shop when I saw Detective Fleming coming in the front. Your friend, Meredith, helped me out."

"Yeah, she's a good one. What'd she do?"

"For one thing, she left *her* back door unlocked, too. I scrambled in there, got a cup of coffee, and had just seated myself and scalded my tongue gulping when Fleming came in through the front. I wanted it to look like I'd been there awhile. Anyway, Meredith gave me an alibi meant to make him think I'd been sitting there drinking coffee for an hour. I owe her."

"That's how life spins for most of us down here. We have to watch out for one another—as much as we can, anyway—because, usually, no one else does."

"Yeah. Makes you wonder why nobody was watching out for Fiona, doesn't it?"

Lanny sighed. "We do what we can. Evil doesn't always leave footprints."

"Footprints! That reminds me—I went out on a limb, showed the shoeprint to Fleming."

"Yeah?"

"Yeah. He pushed for an explanation as to how I knew about it. I told him not to look a gift horse in the mouth." Dry Rot sprang into Jeff's lap, and he nudged the cat onto the floor. "Turns out a rookie cop made it."

"I'll keep that in mind, in case I end up on trial." Lanny drank from an orange-colored cup, watched Jeff over its rim. "You didn't tell Fleming about the folder, did you?"

"No." Jeff drank more coffee. "Lanny," he began, "I have to be able to find you, to know what you're up to— within reason, of course. It'll be easier for me to continue to vouch for you, if I have a general idea that you're not hiding. We can't get anything done if we're both in jail."

"You're right."

"Where have you been?"

Lanny stared at his shoes. "I got a lead on the majolica. I was following it but it fizzled out."

"Did it ever cross your mind that I could've helped you?"

"No. Besides, you've done enough. I didn't want to bother you."

"Baloney. I already stuck my neck out for you—"

"I didn't ask you to, you know."

Jeff blinked. "I didn't mean it that way. I told you from the beginning I wanted to help. But I can't help if you're going to hide things. Do you want to go to prison for a murder you didn't commit?"

Lanny just shrugged.

"What? All of a sudden you're giving up?" It sounded more desperate than he intended, because his nose had started itching. He sneezed, then rose and walked to the window. "Give me one reason to care, Lanny."

"I'll give you the only reason *I* care. The majolica was my wife's."

FIFTEEN

"YOUR WIFE?" JEFF sat back down. He couldn't have been more surprised if Dry Rot had told him to shut up and listen.

"Ex-wife, actually. Janet and I eloped when we were kids. Well, *legally,* we were kids, so our families hauled us back to the courthouse and had it annulled. The last time I saw Janet, she was being dragged away crying. My parents put me in the back of the limo and took me home."

"Limo?"

Lanny shrugged. "My family had money. Anyway, that night I threw some things into a backpack, and left. I thumbed my way as far as Pennsylvania, bought my old pickup at a used-car lot in Pittsburgh with money I had taken out of savings, and drove west till I hit water."

Jeff recovered, a little. "You could've told me this last week."

"I thought I could handle it."

"So, you've been here ever since you left home?"

"Yeah. I don't know whether my family ever tried to find me. For a long time, I didn't care. I was pretty messed up by the time I arrived out here; got into stuff I shouldn't have, eventually ended up here at the Morrison. After I got my act together, I came up with a plan to contact Janet but, by then, she'd left home, too."

"Now that you've got it together, why do you still live here? Isn't this place more of a layover on the way to better things?"

"Yeah. I was in the process of landing a bona fide apartment when I got arrested." He shook his head. "Two *years* on the waiting list, and they 'uninvited' me."

"Talk to them again after all this is sorted out."

"They've given it to someone else by now." Lanny rubbed his face. "I'll go back to worrying about that after I get out of this mess."

"So," Jeff prompted, "this majolica that you suspected was your wife's turned up at Fiona's?"

"More than suspected. I gave it to Janet as a wedding gift. It had been in my family forever, and she vowed never to let it out of her hands. So, when it showed up at Fiona's shop, I had to have it, trace its provenance, try to find Janet. I don't know if the fact that it showed up on the market means that she was in the area and needed money, or that she's finally stopped caring, or that something has happened to her, or . . . I just don't know. But I have to find out."

"Is this the first time you've tried to find her?"

"I used to try but I didn't really know how to go about it. Then . . . well, years pass, you learn to let go of things. When that majolica surfaced, it made me realize I never got over Janet."

"Lanny, I wish I knew what to say. I'm sorry you've had so much thrown at you."

"That's life. You gotta take it as it comes, or it'll eat you alive."

Jeff juggled several thoughts, dropped one into the conversation. "Describe the item for me. I'll keep an eye out for it, too."

"It's a figural, unmarked, of a farmer in blue overalls standing in a cornfield and holding two baskets by the handles. It's fourteen inches tall, and on the bottom of each basket, the artist painted the initial *J*. That makes it sort of unique. Typically, you won't find markings like that on a piece."

Jeff said, "Do you figure those were the artist's initials? J.J.?"

"Could've been, but that doesn't matter. Don't you get it? The *J*s matched our names: Janet and John."

"Right."

"I grew up with that figurine, kept it in my room when I was a boy, put loose change, marbles, stuff like that in the baskets."

Only when Lanny talked freely while describing the piece, and his attachment for it, did Jeff pick up on the Yankee *R* sound. He'd successfully hidden it before.

Jeff said, "Was there any documentation about all this in the folder?"

"Oh, yeah." Lanny went to the desk and retrieved the accordion file. He took from it a manila envelope, and handed that to Jeff.

Jeff opened the envelope, and pulled out a pair of chipboard rectangles secured all around with paper clips. When he removed the clips and separated the chipboard, a small, aged piece of paper curled into a cylinder shape.

Lanny said, "I had rolled that up and stuck it inside the figurine when I gave it to Janet. It's the provenance."

Jeff read the list, beginning with "John Whitney Smith, London, 1870" (written in Spencerian script with ink the shade of tobacco), right up through the gentle cursive done with a blue fountain pen that read, "John Landon Smith III,

b. 1977." Scrawled below that in black ink was "Janet Landrigan Smith, 1993."

Jeff considered the scenario. "So, Fiona removed this from the piece? Why?"

"That's what I've been trying to figure out. The provenance is history. The buyer would've wanted this, too. I don't understand why Fiona kept it."

"What if the majolica figure is still somewhere in the shop?"

"There's no reason to think it would be. I was willing to pay Fiona's price, and she found someone else willing to pay even more."

"How can you be sure?"

"Because, whoever bought the majolica paid cash. Lots of cash."

"As in, they bought lots of majolica at market value, or paid lots more for a single piece than it was worth?"

"I think," Lanny said, lifting the flap on the accordion file, "they paid *this* much for my farmer." He retrieved a bulging envelope, and handed it to Jeff.

Jeff looked inside, and let out a low whistle. "There has to be two or three grand here."

"Thirty-five hundred."

Jeff dropped his hands, and the loot, in his lap. "But is there any proof that this bought your majolica?"

"It depends on how you look at it. All of the receipts for the week are here. No single item brought in that much, and most of the inventory is accounted for on the corresponding deposit slips. I mean, practically everybody does a little cash under the table, you know. Looks like Fiona did more than her share last week. It *has* to be for the majolica, don't you think?"

"It's definitely a possibility." Jeff rubbed his forehead. "Now, we have to figure out why, consider the reasons for someone to do that."

"Maybe the buyer has more money than sense?" Lanny offered.

"Maybe. Or, is obsessed to the point of madness. Sheila sees some of that in the eBay auctions. People get so caught up in the game it's like they're bidding with Monopoly money."

"What if it's someone willing to gamble, someone with a plan to make a profit at auction. Or he has some information, like he knows a buyer who's looking for something like this in particular, who's willing to pay whatever it takes to get it."

"All of that's possible, I suppose."

"Still," Lanny said, "we're forgetting about the provenance. Why would the buyer pay so much without having that?"

"Maybe Fiona faked a provenance for it," Jeff ventured. "Something . . . embellished?"

"I can't see her taking a chance like that. She'd been in this business long enough to know what happens when you're caught doing that sort of thing."

"You said yourself that things had been tight for her lately. I'll say it again: people gamble."

"I'll give you that, but if she did, what reason would she have to tell me that she'd already sold it?"

Jeff tried to sort his thoughts, puzzled over all the variables. "To . . . I don't know. Maybe she was in on something." Jeff turned this over in his mind. "What if it was a trap, to learn whether you were really the one who'd given it to your wife? What if your wife was using this to find you?"

Lanny shot out of his seat. "What if that's it? And . . . wait. What if Fiona's murder was random?" He fell back onto the couch. "What if she was my only connection to Janet, and now she's gone? I'm back to square one."

"Perhaps someone has a reason to *put* you back at square one? That would be a motive to kill Fiona."

"Like what?"

"I don't know, you tell me."

"I don't know, either. But I do know that I need to figure out what happened to her."

"Who, Janet or Fiona?" Jeff asked.

"Both, don't you think? Because, to find out what happened to Janet, I first need to know what happened to Fiona."

Jeff sighed. "For starters, let's get a photocopy made of your provenance."

"I already did that. Mustang Sally's holding it for me."

"Mustang Sally." Jeff tilted his head. "She's a sneaky one."

Lanny smiled. "So, it *was* you who followed her the other day."

"Not very well. Man, she's fast."

"Yeah, she's not sure what to think of you. I'll let her know it's okay with me if you two talk. The rest is up to you."

SIXTEEN

꧁꧂

"*W*HAT DO YOU know about majolica?"

Blanche sat forward. "You have some majolica?"

Jeff cocked his head. "Why, Blanche, you're tipping your hand."

She stiffened, cleared her throat, fussed with her collar, and, after a moment, exhaled and relaxed a little. "I'm too comfortable with you, Jeffrey. Sometimes I forget that we do business together."

Blanche and Jeff sat at a table in the Cabbage Rose Tearoom on the fourth floor of her antiques mall. A vendor, who had commandeered the neighboring table, prepared various pots of tea for Blanche to sample.

Jeff said, "Any particular reason you seemed so interested that I might have some?"

"Not really. I get requests for it all the time, and I

thought, perhaps, you'd heard from Frenchie. I'm hoping he sells you that sort of thing, too, in addition to furniture."

How is it everyone knows about my visit to Frenchie Hoffman's? "I haven't heard back from him yet."

"I do hope you'll give me first pick," Blanche said. "I've had a number of inquiries for majolica recently, and my stock's rather low."

"Is that typical? The inquiries, I mean?"

"Sure, nothing unusual about that. Well, except for one gentleman who stood out."

"Why's that?"

"Whoever sells to him will make a nice profit, I expect. No quibbling over price."

"Did he say anything else?"

"Not a lot. Just indicated that he was willing to pay whatever it takes to get just the right piece. Again, not uncommon. Of course, you should know that."

"Right. What did the guy look like?"

"Oh, he didn't come in. He called. And, I expect he'll call back if he doesn't locate what he's looking for. They usually do."

Jeff sat back and looked around the large café. Employees tended the few remaining customers after the lunch rush, replenished muffin baskets, served up sandwiches and desserts. "Do you ever feel out of place with all your teas in latte land?"

"Jeffrey, you know I serve coffee, too. Still, you question my personal choice of leaves over beans. There are at least a dozen Asian tearooms and British tea parlors in Seattle—there's even one near your home that offers more than one hundred teas. If I'm going to maintain my reputation for the most variety, I must expand my repertoire. Lord knows I have the space."

True, Jeff thought. Blanche owned two of the largest warehouses in the region, and had converted one of them into this antiques—and tea—emporium.

"There are some teas in this town that cost over two hundred dollars a pound," she said.

"And here I thought you only had to be concerned with insuring the antiques in this place."

She made a noise but didn't take her gaze from a cup of liquid that looked to Jeff like hot water tinged with a drop of weak pekoe. He wasn't sure if her reaction was to his comment or to the notion that she had to taste this pale concoction. "White tea," she said, then looked up. "The new green."

Jeff thought about the majolica, decided to get back on track. "Do they usually ask for something in particular?"

"Tea drinkers? Oh, yes, they're quite specific." Blanche tasted the brew, nodded her approval to the vendor.

"I meant, those looking for majolica?"

"Oh. Some of them, yes. That's why I'm curious about Frenchie's wares. There might be some European majolica in the lot. I have a customer looking for Palissy. You know, the slithering snakes that you'd swear are real." She shivered. "Mostly, though, I have people looking for American-made Etruscan—Griffin, Smith, and Hill, to be specific. But the gentleman who called didn't know that. He said he didn't want 'any of the creepy stuff.' I suggested something with, perhaps, the Seaweed and Shell pattern. He seemed interested."

"I'm with him, actually," Jeff said. "I don't see the appeal of eating rabbit pie from a game pie dish that has a lifelike depiction of the dead rabbit draped across the lid to serve as the handle."

"I've been in the business so long, I don't think of the pieces in terms of their original functions. As you know, I check for maker's marks, damage—most pieces haven't fared well—and whether repairs were done professionally. The popularity of the stuff's on the rise, so the inquiry didn't surprise me. Only the approach. People usually want to see items firsthand."

"That's changed with internet auctions, though, don't

you think?" Jeff said. "There's more of the obsession to locate. And, we've become accustomed to returning things.
Consumers seem willing to take the risk, to believe in the
almighty eBay feedback. It's sure changed things."

"True. I suppose I'm used to my clientele, the ones who
want to touch an item, and determine when they hold it
whether or not they can live without it.

"I've seen this happen time and time again," she continued. "You'll go for months, years even, without hearing
or seeing a particular collectible, then, all of a sudden,
everybody wants it. It's hot again, it's the next big thing. I
always wonder what makes it so. And, more often than not,
I wonder if it's some sort of conspiracy, like the fashion
designers. I swear, they get together and decide which direction they'll go with style, just so they can loot Jane
Consumer season after season."

"Maybe so, Blanche, but the key component in the
equation is the fact that Jane Consumer likes change. You
know that. People get tired of what they're collecting, or
they amass everything they can find in a particular area,
and they're ready to move on to something different.
Those who move on either buy a bigger house to make
room for the new collectible, or sell off a collection to finance something that'll fit their space when they downsize, or move on to something that can be displayed on the
walls as opposed to tabletops or floor space."

"Well, if majolica is the next hot thing, it could explain
Fiona's change of mind when Lanny returned to pick up
the stuff she was supposed to hold for him." Blanche
sipped tea and grimaced, gave the vendor a thumbs-down.
"I don't agree with those tactics, mind you, but given the
right circumstances, I can see Fiona Brock pulling a stunt
like that."

Jeff hadn't known that Lanny had told Blanche anything about his dealings with Fiona. If Lanny had been one
of Fiona's main suppliers, as Jeff was Blanche's, he hated
to think that she'd sell him out. Blanche was right, though:

Everything depended on the character of the person. They say everyone has a price. Jeff had never bought into that until he'd almost lost Sheila at the hands of someone who was supposed to be a friend. He'd learned then: Price and currency are two very different things.

Blanche tapped her pencil's eraser on her notepad, then made a notation. "Do your questions have anything to do with Lanny's arrest?"

Jeff considered how much to reveal. He wished he knew exactly what Lanny had told Blanche. "It's hard to say. Maybe. Remember when Lanny called my house from jail? He told you that the stuff he was buying for me was gone, too?"

"That's right! Don't tell me it never showed up."

"It didn't. Hasn't. It was some majolica I was buying for Sheila." He gave her a description of the wall turtle and lily-pad basin.

"I'll let my staff know to alert me if anything like that comes in."

"Thanks, Blanche."

Blanche nodded again when the vendor held up two more packages, then she directed Jeff's attention to the large parament cabinet whose nearly four dozen drawers were once used to store communion items. He'd found the piece for her when she'd first opened the tearoom. "Jeffrey, I'm running out of space. Keep an eye out for another chest, would you?"

"Will do." He hoped he might find one. His profit would make a nice-sized dent in the forthcoming winter's heating bill.

"Where were we?" Blanche said. "Oh, yes. You know I'll help Lanny any way I can."

"I know. And you know what the snoop game's like. You question every little thing, just in case. Typically, I'd say ninety percent of it is thrown out. But supposing it has something to do with Lanny, what've you got? Any other details about any of the people who have been inquiring?"

"Nothing I can think of, offhand."

"Tell you what. I'll have Detective Chris Fleming get in touch with you, just in case. He might want you to call the police department if anyone else contacts you looking for majolica."

SEVENTEEN

∽≺◊≻∽

*A*ND CALL SHE did.

"Your friend, Mrs. Appleby," Fleming said by way of greeting when Jeff answered the phone three days later, "is on a first-name basis with every cop in her precinct. Dispatch sends a unit every time she calls but I don't know how we can keep it up at this rate."

"How many times?"

"Five. So far."

"Since Monday?" Jeff couldn't imagine so many people contacting Blanche's shop specifically for majolica.

"That's right. Of course, I've been away from the office for an hour. You might want to add one or two more to that total."

"Any of them pan out?"

"Nope. It's the boy who cried wolf. Over and over and over . . ."

"It beats missing a real lead on a killer, doesn't it?"

"That's what I keep telling my officers. And myself."

"Has she turned any of them on to collecting?"

"She told you, didn't she?"

Jeff chuckled. "No, I just know Blanche. Her enthusiasm is contagious."

"You got that right. Remember Holcomb from the crime scene? He bought two vintage Harley-Davidson oil cans. And one of the female cops bought several handkerchiefs with daisies on them." He made a noise. "Go figure. Toughest cop I've got, and she bought yellow-daisy hankies."

Jeff had witnessed more astonishing unions than that one. He said, "Maybe it reveals she has compassion, Detective."

"I suppose," he said distractedly. "Actually, I called to talk to Sheila. Is she busy?"

Jeff missed a beat before responding. "Hang on, let me check."

He carried the cordless to the conservatory, where Sheila was tending her herb garden. "Detective Fleming for you."

She grinned as she took the phone. "Chris? Hi!" Pause. "Yes, I'm excited, too." Another pause. "Of course . . . Yes, I'll plan for either day . . . Thanks, you, too."

She pressed the Off button, handed the phone back to Jeff, and went back to work.

"What?" Jeff said. "You got a date with the young detective?"

"Are you jealous?"

"I would be, if I thought it were true."

"Good." She kissed him lightly. "Actually, Chris is bringing his mother over to visit me one afternoon next week, probably Thursday. But he wanted to let me know that his schedule might change that, give or take a day. I'll adjust."

"I thought his mom was agoraphobic, too."

"She is, only she's had a breakthrough recently."

Jeff hoped it was contagious. "I'll try to stay out of your way, then."

"Don't be silly." She placed freshly snipped greens into a small basket and went back toward the house proper.

He followed her to the kitchen. "It smells great in here. New recipe?"

"Yes." She washed a handful of the herbs, then mixed them into a pot of other ingredients on the range-top.

Jeff thought it looked like stuffing. "What's your secret ingredient?"

"Parrot," she said. "They're really hard to work with."

He tried to remember how many birds he'd seen in the conservatory when it hit him. "My Favorite Year," he said, identifying the movie she quoted from. "Do I win a prize?"

"You can taste this, if you want, but it's for the birds."

It took him a second to grasp her meaning. "You mean to tell me you're cooking gourmet for them?"

She spread the concoction on a baking sheet to cool. "I thought I'd try a recipe from one of the bird magazines. If they don't eat it, we can have it for dinner."

Before he could determine if she was joking, the phone rang. It was still in his hand, so he answered it.

"Jeffrey," Blanche said, "I may have something."

"What's that?"

"Do you remember when I told you about the man who phoned about majolica?"

"Yeah, sure."

"Well, Trudy's been going through the caller ID, erasing old numbers on the phone's display. She came across a call from the Monaco that you might be interested in."

"The Hotel Monaco?"

"Yes. It was made the day Fiona was killed. She remembered it as the actual date Lanny was arrested, because it was also the date of your birthday party."

Jeff wondered whether Fleming was right about

Blanche crying wolf. "I'm sure you get dozens of calls every day. Why does this one seem important?"

"It's the only one that stands out. Trudy's been cross-checking, and every other call that day was from either a local residence or one of our regulars."

"Have you called Detective Fleming?"

"Of course, but . . . Jeffrey, the dispatcher acts like I'm her boyfriend's mother or something. She said that it probably didn't mean anything but that she'd tell him when he comes in."

"Did you tell her it's not her job to screen evidence?"

"I tried to but I didn't get very far."

"I'll track him down. How long will you be there?"

"I'll wait until one of you calls me back."

They rang off, and Jeff retrieved Fleming's cell phone number from his own caller ID.

The detective picked up on the first ring.

Jeff said, "Little Red Riding Hood just called looking for her woodsman."

Fleming sighed into the phone. "What's her number?"

Jeff rattled off the exchange for All Things Old. "Don't tell her I called her that. I have to work with her."

"So do I, it seems. Thanks, Talbot."

Curiosity got the best of Jeff. He looked up the Monaco's address, and drove downtown.

Detective Fleming had moved fast. By the time Jeff entered the lobby of the plush hotel, Fleming was finishing up with the clerk at the registration desk.

"No luck?" Jeff said as Fleming turned.

"You just can't stay away from it, can you?" Fleming sighed.

Jeff waited.

Fleming came around. "I've got them pulling records and security tapes. This is the perfect place for a kid, though, if you have the bucks. The Monaco provides a pair of goldfish for your room upon request. Kids love it."

Jeff said, "What do kids have to do with it?"

"Just something in a surveillance tape from the vic's shop that I'm following up on. The Edgewater is good, too. A teddy bear on every bed."

Jeff waited a beat, hoping the detective would elaborate on the tape's content. When he didn't, Jeff said, "If you have the bucks for a place like this."

"Precisely." Fleming glanced at the desk, where three employees—two male, one female—processed guests. A third clerk spoke in hushed tones to a man in his fifties who wore a managerial air. They glanced up at the detective.

"There's my cue. Let me know if you come across anything." He walked away, effectively telling Jeff to get lost.

⟨⟩⟩

The Talbots spent the next three days in their usual routine, Sheila working on the auction business, calling meetings with Jeff about how much more product she'd like to have for the remainder of the year, poring over cookbooks in search of recipes for her visit from Fleming's mother, and fussing over Morty, Bargain Basement, and Poe.

Jeff's routine included mapping out areas to go picking, tending bookkeeping chores, catching up on antiques research, and fussing with Morty, Bargain Basement, and Poe.

It wasn't enough to busy his mind and prevent him from contemplating Lanny's situation. He picked up the phone a hundred times, re-cradled it a hundred times. He debated whether to call the old baker, whether to call Walcher at the Morrison, whether to try again to find Mustang Sally, whether to call Blanche. At one point, he even considered calling Fleming, just to see if he could weasel any info on the hotel angle. And he cursed himself for getting hooked on a case. Again.

EIGHTEEN

~~~~~

*F*RENCHIE HOFFMAN CALLED on Monday.

Jeff had finished lunch, and was about to head down around Cle Elum for some rough-and-tumble country picking when the phone rang. He'd had the receiver in his grip so much over the weekend he was surprised not to find the darn thing there now. He recovered quickly, and grabbed it before the second ring.

"Frenchie here, Talbot. Sorry to leave you hanging fire but I had to cross the pond, take care of some family business. You been to Europe lately?"

"Not for several years." Jeff didn't care if the man had been to the moon and back, he was *back*. He was alive, he was home, and he was calling Jeff. He was going to sell.

"I always enjoy the visit," Frenchie said, "but I enjoy getting back here more."

"I understand. Glad to hear that you're well."

"Why wouldn't I be?" Without pausing for an answer, Frenchie said, "Son, your suggestion made things so simple it was scary. You plant that idea with enough people, and you won't go begging. The trip back to Europe helped, too; made me see things in a whole new light. How soon can we do this?"

"I can be there by two, if that's what you want."

"Bring your checkbook. And a moving van."

Jeff didn't know whether the man meant a moving van as in Two Men and a Truck or a moving van as in United Van Lines. He made a quick call to Blanche, got the phone number of the guys she used for big jobs, and phoned to make arrangements.

"Physical Conveyors, Incorporated, Melissa speaking."

Jeff said, "Oh. I'm looking for movers."

"Movers and Shakers, that's us. Well, umm"—nervous laugh—"that's not us. That name's been taken. We're now called Physical Conveyors. We convey your stuff, physically."

"Yes, I get what it means," Jeff said, wondering if anyone at Physical Conveyors had noticed the similarity between their new name and *Politically Correct.* Since he was in a hurry, he didn't bother to point it out. "I need to arrange for some help this afternoon."

He sorted details, gave Melissa the directions, waited while she read them back, and confirmed their arrival at Hoffman's for three o'clock. He grabbed checkbook and cell phone, and drove toward Steilacoom.

～～～

Hoffman greeted him at the door holding a feather duster. "I couldn't reach my housekeeper to come in for a touch-up. Heck, what I've paid her to dust and wax all this wood for years . . . anyway . . . " Hoffman shook his head, then led Jeff through the house a room at a time, pointing at one piece and then another, arching a brow with each one.

Each time, Jeff named a price, Hoffman gave a nod, Jeff tallied, and Hoffman looked it over.

The old man mopped his forehead with a handkerchief. "That's enough dough to keep my heart pumping another decade or two."

When it was all said and done, Jeff had purchased three of the four bedroom suites ("only need one to sleep on, and I haven't had any company since Kennedy was president"); a parlor set consisting of divan, love seat, and six chairs that were crammed into one of the bedrooms; a dozen accent tables; two linen-covered dress forms with large metal hoopskirts; and two Barrister bookcases, full of various French volumes, Victorian books of flowers and poetry, and a ten-volume set of *Draper's Self-Culture* printed in 1913. Jeff would make enough profit to keep his own household running for months.

That's how he liked it, if he could make it work. None of this crack-of-dawn hovering, grabbing smalls, elbowing your way through crowds.

After sending the Physical Conveyers to Blanche's with the load, Jeff returned to his car. He picked up his cell phone to call Sheila (he'd left it in the car, so as not to be interrupted while crunching numbers with Hoffman), but the screen read No Service. He'd try her after he got back to the city.

He rolled toward All Things Old, soon to learn that while he'd been an hour from home, Blanche had been serving tea and tidbits to a man and his daughter.

NINETEEN

❦

W HEN JEFF ARRIVED behind Blanche's antiques shop, he had to wait while the moving van loaded with Frenchie's stuff wedged itself between the police units that were nosed haphazardly up to the loading dock.

He jumped from the woodie, shot up the cement stairs and into the back entrance.

Officer Holcomb was on his way out. He stopped, identified Jeff. "You're that guy from the other place over in Pioneer Square."

"That's right. What's going on?"

"Fleming's been trying your cell phone. You'll find him in Ms. Appleby's office."

"Is she okay?"

"She's fine." Holcomb grinned, started again toward the exit. "I told Fleming he should deputize her."

Jeff hurried down the corridor, passing another uni-

formed cop on the way. In the office, Blanche and Fleming
sat in front of twin television/VCR combos. They leaned in
close to the small screens while Fleming juggled remotes,
hit Play, Rewind, then Play again. The image on the left
screen jumped.

Jeff said, "Double-feature at Blanche's Bijou. Where's
the popcorn?"

Blanche popped up from her chair as soon as she heard
his voice. "Jeffrey, he was here!"

"Who was here?"

"The gentleman I told you about—the one who had
phoned about majolica."

"Why is he any different from all the other callers?"

"Here." Fleming pointed to the screen where he had ad-
justed the picture. "I'll need to take both tapes to headquarters, have CSI check them on their high-tech toys, but
it looks to me like we have a match."

Jeff leaned in. Pictured on the screen to the right was a
man and a girl having tea in Blanche's Cabbage Rose. The
screen on the left showed another antiques shop—he recognized it as Fiona's—and a girl, about nine or ten years
old, seated on the floor playing with a cat. Dry Rot.

"When was that one filmed?" Jeff said, indicating the
one with Dry Rot in the picture. This would be the tape
Fleming mentioned in the Monaco's lobby.

"Friday, October tenth," said Fleming. "The evening
before the murder."

"You think it's the same girl?"

"Seems to be," Fleming said. "The hair's different but
that's so easily changed you learn to look past it. She has
the same features, same mannerisms."

"Why, of course it's her," Blanche said. "The gentle-
ness, and that cautious little smile before she warms up to
you." She stared at the screens another second before turning her gaze to Jeff. "Still, I just can't believe her father
would harm anyone. He was so charming and clean-cut
and educated. Very good with the girl, too."

"How so?"

"He was so patient, and he really listened to what she said. He didn't dismiss her like so many parents do their children. Allison seemed completely comfortable with him. I must admit I was a bit nervous about calling the police on him. I'm not a very good Miss Marple."

Jeff thought how Blanche would make a great Miss Marple, if she toned down the hair color. "He's been in town awhile then."

Fleming stood. "Or lives here. Or comes and goes."

"You did the right thing, Mrs. Appleby," he continued. "You're sure he didn't give you his name?"

"I'm afraid not. I mean, I'm sure he didn't. The girl told me her name was Allison. I started to ask his name but an item caught his eye, and he stepped away to get a better look. That's when the girl started telling me everything she knew about majolica. We never got back to names.

"When he returned from looking around the shop," Blanche went on, "he said he wanted to find some majolica for the girl's mother. A gift."

"Anything in particular?"

"He was specific about what he *didn't* want. He said that he wasn't interested in anything with animals, or cupids, or satyrs."

"Satyrs?" Fleming looked blank.

"Lecherous ogres with horns. Their faces were used as masks on many of the majolica urns. He said perhaps a figurine. Something pastoral."

"You'll have to help me out again, Mrs. Appleby."

"Of course. It means tranquil, serene."

Jeff considered giving Fleming an antiques word-of-the-day calendar for Christmas. To Blanche, he said, "That sounds like the same guy you told me about the other day. And, from the looks of this tape, Fiona knew this guy."

Jeff and Fleming exchanged glances. Fleming said, "Could be the same piece that Fiona Brock allegedly sold out from under Smith."

"Sure sounds like it. But why? And, how is it that he knows about it, too?"

Fleming said, "Could be that they were in on some sort of a scam."

Blanche said, "I simply reported their visit because I told you I would. However, if this were the man you're looking for, I don't think he'd be so blatant as to have his daughter studying majolica. She had read of the majolica in the newspaper, and—"

"You mean," Jeff said, "he lets his daughter read about murder?"

"Heavens, no! She was skimming the paper as a vocabulary assignment. When she came across 'majolica,' she asked him what it was. He told me that he didn't know much about it, so he gave her a history assignment, and that's why they're going around learning what they can. It seems they got hooked, and that's why he's looking to purchase some."

Jeff glanced at the TV screen. "Why wasn't the girl in school?"

"I asked the same thing," Blanche said. "Shows how old-school I am, as it were. She's homeschooled. She should make an A in history. She knew about everything from the Italian shipping port of Majorca—that's how the pottery got its name—to the exquisite European pieces, to how the American potters struggled with consumers who were hooked on the European designs, and how those potters had to make exact copies of the imports in order to make any sales at all. Good thing I wasn't busy this morning. It was encouraging, though, to hear a youngster so excited about history and antiques."

"Very enlightening." Fleming jotted notes in his pad.

Blanche turned her chair away from the TV sets, and seated herself at her desk. "The girl even knew that Charles Darwin was the grandson of none other than Josiah Wedgwood, and how, after his evolution theories were made public, the Victorians went nuts over the majolica teapots that sported monkeys—effectively putting them in their rightful place. That led to my mentioning the teapot collection in the Cabbage Rose. When I told her that one of the monkey teapots is on display there, she couldn't get up there fast enough."

Jeff said, "I've never thought much of homeschooling, but if a parent takes that approach, it's a cool way to learn. Obviously, the kids retain more that way."

"Oh, I think so," Blanche said. "They're being exposed to a three-dimensional world, as opposed to simply reading about it in textbooks."

Fleming put away the notepad. "I've been checking hotels for father-daughter pairs ever since I first saw the tape of that girl with the cat a couple of weeks ago. Apparently, fathers and daughters traveling together aren't as uncommon as you might think."

Blanche poured tea from a pot in a rose chintz cozy. "Why do you say that?"

"We've turned up four so far, and that's just from the hotels. We've also interviewed museum staff, checked school activities, homeschooling, all that. What with more women working, and more people in general either working at home or working swing shifts so they can stagger child care, the stay-at-home dad is becoming more and more common."

"Did either of you want tea?" Blanche hoisted her eyebrows and the pot.

Both men declined.

Jeff said, "How can child care be that expensive? The kids are in school much of that time, right?"

"Sure," Fleming said, "but if you don't want a latchkey kid, you end up paying someone to pick them up and take them to day care. Some schools offer a before- and after-school service but it costs almost as much as full-time day care. Believe me, I've seen enough situations with kids home alone to know that I'll never subject a child of my own to it."

"I didn't agree with the espresso tax proposal," Blanche admitted, "but I hope a logical solution to the day-care problem is found soon."

"Back to those hotels," Jeff said. "Did you turn up anything suspicious?"

"No, but I'll check back where we got the previous hits, have records check dates of stays, too—not only the different names that come up."

"You think the guy is hotel hopping, or returning to somewhere he's stayed recently, to mix it up?"

"It would explain some things."

Fleming popped the surveillance tapes from the VCRs. "I'll have to keep your tape for now, Mrs. Appleby."

"Certainly."

"You've been a tremendous help." Fleming took a business card from his breast pocket and handed it to Blanche. "Call me directly if you think of anything else."

"I will. Do you think he'll come back?" Blanche didn't seem fearful but, rather, like someone who liked to plan ahead.

"Doubtful," Fleming said. "If he is our suspect, he realizes that he can be recognized, and I'm sure he's left town already. If he's not our guy, then you have nothing to—"

"Oh!" Blanche interrupted. "I just remembered something but I don't know if it's of any importance."

"Go ahead."

"He went to the men's room. While he was gone, Allison confided in me that she hoped they found a pretty piece of majolica for her mother because it would mean that her dad was trying to win her back. Allison said they had divorced earlier this year.

"When he returned," Blanche continued, "he asked if the girl had been bothersome. I sensed her concern that I would betray her trust, so I told him that I'd been teaching her about English tea rituals. He started to quiz her, so I threw out some quick bits. Then, he said there would be a bonus if the exchange was kept confidential. I thought he meant about the tea, and my confusion must've been obvious because he clarified by saying that he meant a majolica exchange. A purchase, you see. I didn't suspect anything regarding that, as I have several clients who prefer anonymity. Typically, it's with rare pieces, but I *never* question the request."

Fleming said, "He should've paid you the bonus."

"What on earth for? I didn't sell him anything."

"Ah, but you weren't bound to confidentiality, either."

Blanche raised a brow. "Ah, indeed."

Jeff let that sink in, then both men told Blanche good-bye.

Out back, Jeff said to Fleming, "Have any other surveillance tapes from Fiona's shop surfaced from that Saturday?"

"No, this is it." Fleming stared at the tapes in his hand. When he looked up, his expression clearly told that he was onto something. "I've been operating on the notion that the victim stashed this tape as proof that Smith had fought with her. But there was a call from the Monaco to Fiona Brock's shop that afternoon, an hour or so after the fight. Now I think it has something to do with the man and the girl, and the hotel lead."

"The Monaco?" Jeff asked.

"Yeah. We learned that two calls from the Monaco were made to Brock's number: the first one the day before her murder, the second one the afternoon of."

"How long have you known that?"

"Not long enough. You see, Brock had one phone line but no caller ID screen on the shop phone. I sent a couple of guys back over to double-check phones in her living quarters upstairs. They found the base to a cordless on the floor just under the bed by the headboard. It was hidden by a pile of clothes. They finally located the phone itself in a drawer in the bathroom vanity."

Jeff remembered that Blanche had called Fiona an old

bat the night of his party. "Was she showing signs of dementia?"

"Not if you're basing it on the phone bit. I see it all the time, people putting their cordless phones down everywhere you can think of. Not only in the house but also in their garages, their yards, storage sheds, you name it.

"By the time they found Brock's phone," he went on, "the battery was long dead. They had to put it on its base and wait for some juice before they could check the caller ID display."

Jeff thought back to the eleventh, and until that instant hadn't equated Fiona Brock's murder with his birthdate. While the murder seemed to have just happened, the memories of his birthday party were distant, like it had taken place months earlier. He said, "I drove Lanny down to Pioneer Square late that afternoon."

"What time was that?"

"Between four and four-thirty, as I recall. He was going to the bank first, before purchasing the majolica. At the time, I didn't know who from. What are you considering?"

Fleming said, "Maybe the vic's partner in crime told her that she'd better not have any surveillance equipment running. She told him she didn't—"

"But," Jeff said, "too late, she remembered that she'd taped his visit the night before."

"Exactly. So, she hid this tape, and we were fortunate enough to find it."

"Where'd you find it?"

"Under the plastic liner on the cat's litter box."

TWENTY

❦

*I*T WAS LIKE taking the Seattle Walking Tour while on speed.

Jeff had spotted Sally coming out of Boomtown Café, her height grabbing his attention, and her camel coat and Burberry scarf confirming the tag. This time, she wore a sock hat knitted of variegated yarn in muted earthtones with twin points sticking up on top of her head that put him in mind of gazelle horns.

With only three days till Halloween, he'd gone to Pioneer Square to take one more stab at landing cool costumes. Sheila assured him that she had a Plan B, but he wanted to nose around for Mustang Sally anyway. Still, when he spotted her, it startled him.

He strapped himself into undercover mode and followed. Trotting up and down hills, he kept her in his sights as she hurried east, then south.

She moved fast but not like before, not like someone fleeing pursuit. Jeff hung back, more careful this time.

His target took a right at the corner near the Smith Tower. Jeff picked up his pace, passed a cigar store, and trailed with him the aromas of sweet tobacco.

His mark bolted right at the corner, and he couldn't be sure but thought she'd made him. Once she was out of sight, he pulled a Seahawks cap from his windbreaker pocket and snugged it on his head, then shucked the reversible jacket, turning it from gray sweatshirt fabric to navy nylon in a matter of seconds. Easy, cheesy, and he had a disguise. His old partner Gordy would have been proud.

As if he'd teased fate, it started raining.

He spotted Sally a half block ahead on the other side of the street.

The young woman looped, ducked, and dodged her way in and out of foot traffic, under awnings, around corners, and from what Jeff's nose told him, past every coffee shop in latte land. He lost his bearings until he surfaced geographically under the pergola at Pioneer Square, and caught a glimpse of the gazelle moving east.

He pursued as she ate up block after block of sidewalk, descended stairs, and wove around tables and chairs at Waterfall Garden Park. The chilly air carried on it the pleasant aromas of ginger and steeped tea. Then, as quick as you can say sayonara, all of his senses were in the East.

The International District. Jeff hadn't been over here in a long time, and it took effort to focus on the subdued shades of Sally's outfit among the shiny flashes of Ming red, lacquer black, and polished gold.

He picked up bits of conversation in Japanese as he walked, along with music plucked in minor keys and accented by reverberating gongs, and the *clack-clack* of bamboo wind chimes that dangled from buildings with pagoda-style roofs.

Occasionally, in his home, he heard Lucy and Polly

speak in Japanese to each other as they worked. Now, he wondered what the sisters were like when they were down here, surrounded by their own culture.

Sally stopped under the wall of origami art at the bus stop, lit a cigarette she'd pulled from a fanny pack strapped around her waist, then continued east-southeast.

She walked several blocks before stopping in front of a store window. Jeff did the same. His gaze lighted on a newspaper tearsheet from the early 1900s, folded to showcase an ad offering tea, rice, and opium for sale. He glanced at other items in the window: antiques. He gazed at the ad, clenched his jaw. He checked on Sally (she hadn't moved), then went back to the ad. He knew a guy in San Francisco who collected opium pipes, and this scrap of ephemera might be right up his alley. And, Jeff couldn't do a thing about it.

Other items in the display caught his eye. A ginger jar, a pair of exquisite cloisonné boxes, a delicately embroidered scarf—all of it out of his reach for today.

Something about the boxes looked familiar, and he realized there was one like them in his own house. His home reflected every aspect of Victoriana, including many items of Asian influence. Oriental rugs, ginger jars, and silk screens were in virtually every room of his home. He'd never given them much thought, had merely accepted them because they'd always been there. But now he recognized their beauty, their history.

Next to him, a young couple stood in front of an iron gate, struggling with buttons on a box that presumably would allow entrance if one entered the correct combination. The woman studied the slip of paper in her hand, then quietly said to her companion, "No, see? Punch these three numbers, then turn the knob and open the gate at the same time."

He replied, "Is that one five, or five one, before the two?"

"Five, one," she answered, seemingly oblivious to the

junkie who perched on the building's brick lip four feet from them and spouted a maniacal version of the "secret" code to the gate's lock. "Five! One! Two!" escaped in spurts from the man's lips as his body jerked uncontrollably. The skeletal man gripped his knees as if attempting to prevent his body from exploding into a thousand shards of glass. "To the right!" he spat. "No! Five! One! Two! To the left! Turn the knob! Five! One! Two!"

Jeff stared, spellbound. When he broke free, shame over his indiscretion gave way to pity, and he wished he could do something to help the guy. But he knew that if he gave a handout while the man was in this state, it would only be lost to a mugger or a dealer.

He glanced down the street, saw Sally rounding the corner at the end of the block. Jeff left the strung-out man to his self-assigned rendition of hell-work.

He committed to memory his location, and hoped he might be able to return for that newspaper. As he wove his way through the crowds like a silk thread in a kimono, he wondered whether any of his ancestors had walked the dark side of old Chinatown and its opium dens.

Sally reached the next corner and glanced back. Jeff had anticipated the move, and had stepped into the alcove of a storefront. He counted to four, chanced a peek. She was practically ambling. She turned left at the next corner without looking back. Jeff picked up his pace.

When he fell in beside her a block and half later, he said by way of greeting, "Seen Lanny lately?"

She didn't try to run but she didn't stop walking, either. And, she didn't respond.

"Have you known Lanny very long?"

Nothing.

"You've probably known him longer than I have, and I'll wager you know him better. The one thing I do know, though, is that he's not a killer. He—" What? Jeff's mind cast for examples but everything he came up with was off-limits. He couldn't tell her about Lanny's upstanding performance as an informant, about how he'd anonymously helped get countless drug dealers, thieves, and con artists off the streets. He couldn't tell her about the snooping in Fiona's shop, even though it would establish his bond with the young picker. At last, his thoughts landed on something that wasn't off-limits. "Lanny's taking care of Dry Rot, Fiona's cat." *Did that come across as lame as it sounded?*

She stopped. "Is that all you got? A shelter'll do the same thing for ten days, then put it out of its misery."

Yep, lame. Jeff said, "He saved my wife's life once."

"Once? What, she got nine lives or somethin'?"

"Huh?" Jeff tried to explain. "I said he saved my *wife's* life, not—"

"Jeez, calm down. I heard what you said. Why you got business with Lanny?"

Fortunately, Lanny had briefed him on what to say. Unfortunately, this odd mix of paranoia and spunk had thrown him. He backpedaled mentally, tried to determine where he'd been derailed. "He's trying to find the real killer."

"He would be."

Jeff couldn't tell whether she was being sarcastic, or making a character observation. He forged on. "He said you were there when he and Fiona argued."

"Yeah. She didn't do right by him. I mean, if she'd promised to hold something for me, I'd have been ticked off, too."

"Was that like her?"

Mustang Sally chewed at the dead skin on her lip. "No. Maybe, I don't know. Look, I gotta get."

"Wait. Please. Lanny told me a week ago that you'd talk to me. Why the cat and mouse game?"

She stopped, studied his features quickly before looking away, her glance darting everywhere, constantly scanning her surroundings. Jeff knew that she had every detail of his face committed to memory, just in case she needed to describe him to a police sketch artist at some future point.

She blinked water out of her eyes. He realized that he and she were both getting wet from the rain.

"Come on," he prompted. "Why the games?"

She said, "I have to keep my skills sharp. Besides, I wasn't sure it was you."

"You want proof?"

"What do you think?"

He produced his wallet, flipped it open to his driver's license, and kept a tight grip on it while she verified his identity.

When she appeared to be satisfied, he said, "Can I buy you lunch?"

She looked him up and down, then looked up at the Chinese restaurant they stood in front of. Jeff could've sworn one of the painted dragons looked away. "Sure, why not?"

He said, "You like Chinese food?"

"Love it. This kind of place won't let me in, though."

Jeff looked at the restaurant, sized it up as serviceable but nothing fancy. "Yeah, they will. Trust me."

Mustang Sally gave him a look. "Right. Those are two of my favorite words."

He held the door for her, and waited.

She hesitated, and he suspected one of two things: either she wasn't used to manners, or she wasn't keen on someone being behind her.

Finally, though, she took a deep breath and walked inside.

TWENTY-ONE

꧁꧂

*T*HE DINING ROOM was at two-thirds capacity. Most of the customers had already been served, and were now visiting, laughing, enjoying the warm atmosphere. A good sign. If you go into a crowded restaurant and no one's talking, you can bet the service sucks.

Jeff escorted Sally to a booth in the smoking section. He despised eating around smokers, but he remembered enough from his FBI days to know that the nervous young woman would die without a cigarette. At the very least, she'd be easier to get information from if she had her freedoms.

She shucked the coat, and folded it neatly on the booth before sliding in beside it. The cuffs of her black corduroy trousers were frayed, and her red tennis shoes showed extreme wear.

Once seated, she removed her hooded sweatshirt before

digging a cigarette from the fanny pack and lighting up. Jeff counted two more layers: a navy fitted top over a gray ribbed undershirt. Although it appeared stylish (like something his sister-in-law Karen would put together), he suspected that for Sally it was the sum total of her closet. Or, what would be her closet, if she actually had one.

Their server was a no-show till Jeff caught her judgmental glance and motioned her over.

She was a plump girl with black hair and pale skin and looked all of eighteen. She clearly wasn't Asian but had tried for the effect with a heavy dose of black eyeliner extending past the outer corners of her eyes and painted into triangles.

She scuffed her feet as she approached. "We don't serve the homeless in here, and she"—jerk of head—"knows it."

Sally blew a lungful of smoke toward the girl. "Maybe you ought to try it, Miss Piggy. It's a great diet program."

"Ladies," Jeff said warningly. "Actually"—he checked her name tag—"Jude, I own a home. Please bring us two black coffees when you return with our menus. Or, do you need to see my deed?" He flipped open his wallet, retrieved a platinum card that he flashed at her. "Visa." He looked at Sally. "Do we want to be here?"

Sally said, "Probably not. They're gonna spit in your coffee now."

Jeff hated to play his ace, but if it was going to help put Judge Jude in line . . .

He stood, putting his back to Sally, flipped to the back window of the wallet, and discreetly showed his old FBI badge and ID to the server. "I'm here for a good meal and a simple meeting. If there's *any* chance you wouldn't eat it yourself, I'll put a daily visit from the Health Department on your boss's schedule so fast he'll think he's won the lottery from hell." He stopped for breath. "Now. Are we going to have a problem getting proper service?"

"No, sir." Jude forced a smile. "I'll see if that fresh pot is done brewing. Sir."

After the server left and Jeff sat down, Sally said, "Last time I got a prize out of box of Cracker Jacks, it was a lousy tattoo of a daisy. How'd you rate the sudden *nice* from her?"

Jeff moved a shoulder. "I'm former FBI."

Sally started to bolt.

He grabbed her hand. "I said former. Trust me, I'm far removed but the badge usually settles down the ingrates."

"You're pretty handy with that 'trust me' line, aren't you?"

Jeff ignored the question and Sally didn't press.

Jude returned with two steaming mugs of coffee, two menus, and a report of the specials. Without looking at the menu or the waitress, Sally said, "The duck special sounds good to me. Some rangoon, too."

"Make that two," Jeff said.

Jude nodded, shuffled away.

Sally smoked cigarettes like the potheads Jeff had seen when he was an agent: shoulders hunched, holding on to the smoke for dear life. Only difference was that this smoke didn't relax her, didn't mellow out her high-strung characteristics, didn't suppress her fidgeting. She frowned and squinted. She fanned smoke away from bloodshot eyes. She picked at bits of tobacco on her tongue. It added twenty years to her looks.

Jeff said, "I've seen a lot of smokers in my day, but none who looked like they hated it as much as you do. Why don't you quit?"

"These keep me off worse stuff." She rummaged in her fanny pack, unearthed a pack of generic cigarettes and a hotel matchbook, and counted what was left in each.

"How'd you come across that?"

"This?" She held up the gold-foiled pasteboard before fitting it back into the pack along with the smokes, then zipped it. Then she double-checked that she'd zipped it. "I've got a buddy who works at one of the ritzy hotels downtown. He brings me stuff, you know—matches, partial rolls of TP, little jars of ketchup, mustard, jelly. Makes a big difference in my grocery bill at the local Safeway, know what I'm saying?"

Jeff wondered whether anyone had thought of writing a Seattle guidebook about how to survive on the street. Of course, those who were actually doing it weren't your best target audience, and too many of those not doing it didn't care. At least there were people like Tom Walcher at the Morrison, and the DESC's Bill Hobson and his team who were trying to make things better for people like Sally.

"You ain't saying nothin'." She eyed him. "You won't turn him in, will you?"

"Who, your friend? No. Actually, I think it's ingenious, the things you can do—the general you, I mean—to keep going. I'm impressed."

"And I'm freaked. Never met anyone quite like you."

"I've been told that I'm pretty hip for a middle-aged suit."

"You just blew it by using 'hip.'"

Jeff had thought "hip" was back in. Now, he didn't know whether it was, or whether she was pulling his leg. He didn't ask, only because he didn't want to use the phrase "pulling my leg," which probably *was* dated, and then be told that he was getting older by the minute. "Where does your friend live?"

"Who, Wash?"

Wash?

She read his face, said, "Short for Washington. He used to live at the Morrison. Helps a lot of people, know what I'm saying?"

Jeff nodded. "So, you have an apartment at the Morrison?"

"That's not what I said. I crash there from time to time."

Jeff remembered hearing that there were several cots put out each night for the homeless. He wondered if that was what she meant, or if she had different friends throughout the building who allowed her to bunk on their couches.

"Wash hops the free bus every day. Seattle's got it goin',
you know? At first, I came out here because it was about as
far away from New York as I could get. It wasn't till after I
got here that I learned it's tolerable." She patted the fanny
pack. "Of course, everybody needs a plan."

Jeff needed to know whether Fleming had found her but
he didn't want to scare her off. "So, Sally, has anyone
talked to you about the day you bought your coat?"

Her expression told him that she saw right through his
feeble approach. "In other words, have I been questioned in
the murder of Fiona Brock." She blew smoke at him. "Yes,
Detective, we had a wonderful little chat last night.
Happy?"

He wrapped his hands around his cup to take the chill
off. "Doesn't matter to me one way or the other, unless it
helps Lanny. And gets Detective Fleming off my back. His
take was that I'd scared you away last week when you led
me on that clever goose chase. He didn't appreciate my attempt to help, and I don't need him on my case."

She smiled like the Cheshire cat, then shrugged. "I told
him everything I know about that day. There's nothing *mysterious* about any of it, so I don't suppose it'll hurt to throw
you a bone." She recounted what she'd seen at Fiona's antiques shop that afternoon, and other than not noticing
much about the man in the cap, her account matched what
Lanny had told him.

Not much to go on, was right. Jeff said, "Do you know
anything about the majolica she'd promised him?"

Sally said, "Yeah, Fiona was always curious about
Lanny's obsession with that ugly stuff."

"Did she call it ugly, or is that your take?"

"My take, although she wasn't in love with the stuff, either, except if she could make some good bucks on it.
Lanny was always looking for majolica, and Fiona knew it.
But she saw it more as an obsession he couldn't afford to
feed. He always studied the pieces when she first got them
in the shop, admired them, commented on which company

made what piece, or shared the history of a particular design. Weird, when you think about it: Fiona learned most of what she knew about that kind of pottery from Lanny."

Jeff said, "Yeah, weird."

Their food was brought out by someone other than Jude. Jeff took it as a good sign. He watched as Sally curtained herself around her plate, and considered the ways in which the homeless reinvented themselves in order to survive the streets. What manners were unlearned in the interest of eating your food without having it stolen from you? What concessions were made to dignity?

Sally paused, looked up at him. She'd read his mind. "You lose it slowly."

"What's that?"

"All of it—the manners, training, education. The dignity. It starts as a means of fitting in with the others, then moves to protection, or a way to expunge all ties to your own past—a way of erasing the people who hurt you. Eventually, through repetition, it becomes habit. If you try to go back to that exact moment when you changed, you can't pinpoint it."

"But the foundation is still there, I'd think."

She shrugged. "Who knows? I hope I get to test that theory someday."

Sally dipped rangoon in sweet-and-sour sauce. "Everyone's susceptible, you know."

Jeff's skepticism must have been evident on his face, because Sally said, "Okay, I'll prove it. What's the most important thing in your life?"

"That's easy. My wife."

"What if she died? Or disappeared?"

Jeff's chest tightened. He'd been there, didn't want to think about it, didn't want to go back.

"Scary, huh?"

"She was kidnapped a few years ago. Fortunately . . . well, it could've ended up a lot worse than it did."

"If she'd never been found, you might've gone off the

deep end . . . stopped working, stopped paying bills, stopped eating, stopped caring."

"I hadn't thought that far. I didn't have to, thanks to Lanny. I owe him. And, whether he realizes it or not, he's up against it unless we can find out who killed Fiona."

"Yeah," she said quietly.

Jeff watched Sally, pictured what she might have been like before her addiction had cost her everything. It put him in mind of *My Man Godfrey,* a movie made around 1936, and he realized that there's really nothing new under the sun. Godfrey had been a successful businessman, had fallen on hard times, had faced those who treated him a level or two below human. Nowadays, there was more awareness about the homeless, more people were trying to help them now than ever before. But even that needed a hefty dose of knowledge. Jeff knew that what Sally said was true: Given the right circumstances, anyone might find himself in her situation. Or Lanny's. Or Fiona's. Justice wasn't always swift, or even steady. Sometimes, the only justice one got came in a Tom Walcher package: exhausted, and living hand-to-mouth in an often thankless job.

Sally finished eating, and pushed her plate away. "Like I said before, Fiona did a real number on Lanny. I told her that, too."

"You told her? When?"

"Later that day. Didn't I tell you that? I was walking by, saw her at the register and no one was in the shop, so I went in."

"How'd she react to that?"

Sally grunted. "How do you think? Defensive, tried to justify herself."

"Did you tell the cops that?"

"I told that detective, the one I talked to yesterday. I don't have anything to hide. But that was all there was to it. Some guy came in, and she pulled herself together and told me to hit the road, that he was a *real* customer." She grunted again. "And after I'd bought my coat from her that same day."

Sally propped her foot up in the booth, and Jeff said, "I noticed your shoes. Aren't they the kind with the zippered pockets?"

"Kangaroos. I'm into pockets instead of grocery carts. You never know when you're going to need something, when you won't be able to score a bed for the night."

Jeff was doubtful. "Those pockets aren't more than a couple of inches wide, and they're on your foot, to boot."

"Is that supposed to be a joke?"

"Huh? Oh. Boot. No." He summed her up. "On first glance, I see a very slim woman with a fanny pack instead of a purse. What could you possibly be carrying that would cover you for a few days?"

She studied him for several seconds. After Jude had re-filled their mugs, Sally said, "If I impress you, will you book me a hotel room for the night?"

"What?"

"It doesn't have to be real fancy. Just a place to take a hot shower, order room service, watch a movie."

"Your friend who works in the hotel can't do that for you?"

She shrugged. "Not very often, and never through the front door. I mean, sure, there are missions where I can shower, or I can borrow a shower from guys like Lanny, guys who don't expect anything in return. But a girl can get a lot of mileage out of a hot bubble soak and a good night's sleep. It would get me through the winter—therapeutically speaking."

He'd never met anyone like her. No telling what she might achieve if she got a second chance, a job with a fu-ture, a conventional life. Maybe, though, that's what she shied away from: convention. Or, maybe she just needed a break or two. "You know what? It's a deal. I'm curious."

"Curiosity killed the cat," she said as she unzipped the fanny pack.

Two minutes later, her arsenal was neatly arranged on the tabletop.

And, to Jeff's surprise, there was barely room left for their mugs. Her secret was that she'd learned how to downsize, had gone travel-minded all the way.

A Bayer aspirin tin from the forties, half-filled with rust-colored tablets he recognized as ibuprofen; a travel-sized pack of Kleenex; two tampons; a small but mighty Swiss Army knife that housed a blade, scissors, tweezers, toothpick, and a key ring; three large keys on said key ring; a three-by-four-inch notepad inside a black vinyl sleeve with a bank's name and logo (once printed in gold foil on the cover and now worn to a shadow); a tiny ink pen, looped in the notepad's spine; a miniature bottle of hand sanitizer; ChapStick (she opened it, grimaced, hesitated, tossed it into the ashtray); travel toothpaste and toothbrush; two cellophane-wrapped toothpicks; an ID similar to the ones he'd seen Walcher checking at the Morrison; a roll of Tums; four individually wrapped breath mints; a flashlight (small enough to take two AAAs); the stub of a candle with a holder and matches ("just in case the batteries go dead in the flashlight"); two extra batteries; four miniature candy bars; a sample vial of perfume; a hotel sewing kit; an almost empty bottle of Visine; a dollar bill, five dimes, two nickels, and a roll of pennies taped shut on the ends.

Jeff surveyed the loot. "Why a roll of pennies?"

"'Cause I can't afford a roll of quarters."

"Makes sense," he said. And, in a way, it did.

She started the process of returning everything to the pack. When she picked up the flashlight, she flashed its beam in Jeff's face.

He complained.

"Hey, I have to check it, make sure it's still working."

"How often do you do that?"

"Check it? Couple times a day."

Jeff considered pointing out that checking it stole enough juice off the back end of the batteries to make the flashlight fail when she might need it most—but he allowed it would do no good to try to tell this girl anything.

"You sure that's it?"

"Oh, wait." She folded her left leg onto the booth's seat, unzipped her shoe's little pocket, and placed one last item on the table: a tiny key. "My buddies know that if anything ever happens to me, this is the key."

Since she hadn't revealed the photocopy of the majolica provenance that Lanny claimed he'd given her, Jeff wondered if it was stashed away in some safe-deposit box with other pertinent papers. "Key to what?"

"Everything okay?" The manager interrupted.

To Sally, Jeff said, "More coffee?"

"I thought we were supposed to get tea and fortune cookies at the end of the meal."

Astute. Jeff grinned.

The manager bowed slightly before departing.

Jeff scanned the table, pointed toward the knife. "Why the three large keys? Relatively speaking, they take up more space than anything."

Before he could say "tai chi," the tip of the center key was an eyelash's width from his nose.

He'd grabbed her wrist—instinct—but not before realizing that she'd stopped of her own volition. She hesitated an extra second, then smiled and pulled free.

He focused on her right hand, which gripped the Swiss Army knife in its palm. The three keys protruded from between her fingers.

"A girl's gotta have protection."

Jeff swallowed. "Impressive."

Jude showed up with the tea not a minute too soon. She snarled up her nose when she saw all the items on the tabletop but left her thoughts unspoken.

Jeff gulped his tea, and hoped it would calm his pounding heart. He swallowed one last time, and said, "What hotel did you have in mind?"

TWENTY-TWO

EMPLOYEES AND GUESTS alike looked at Jeff as if he were a john who, from the looks of the girl he'd picked up, couldn't afford a shoeshine in the place, let alone a room.

Jeff wasn't exactly sure which hotel they'd ended up at after taking advantage of the free bus ride to Seattle's downtown and walking till Sally had entered a door held open by a stunned valet in hat and tails. All Jeff knew was that it was the one where her friend called Wash worked. She had decided to go there while on the bus, even though he had dangled the Monaco's goldfish in front of her.

Sally glided into the lobby as Jeff imagined she had once done down Paris runways.

The young clerk at the registration desk was well-tanned (thirty-days-no-limit package or a week in Cancun, Jeff couldn't tell), with a sparse blond mustache parked over a smirk. Jeff booked a room for the night, and told the young man that the lady was to have free rein of the room service menu through the next day's breakfast. He played his old FBI card for the second time in as many hours, only quicker this round—the kid looked mischievous enough to have seen a badge or two. "If she calls and tells me she's not having a good vacation, I'll be back and I'll bring my friends. Understood?"

"Yes, Mr. Talbot."

He then escorted Sally on a side trip to the gift shop, where a female clerk with the appearance and color of a shriveled green grape didn't bother to greet them. He told Sally to pick out some snacks, magazines, and anything else she might need. While she shopped, he watched the clerk, who alternately looked down her nose at Sally and cleaned smudges from atop the glass case that served as checkout counter.

As Jeff waited, he stood at the glass walls and watched guests moving to and fro through the lobby. A couple with a child walked through, and put Jeff in mind of the father and daughter from Blanche's shop. Anxiety practically got the best of him as he scanned the lobby for father-daughter pairs. Then, he told himself that Fleming would've been the first to know if such a pair had checked in, which would also mean that they would have already been checked out—in more ways than one. He calmed down after that, chalking up his paranoia to too much time spent with Mustang Sally.

At the checkout, Sally placed copies of *Vogue* and *Real Simple* on the counter (a perfect combo, he thought, for a former runway model living the simple life on the streets), along with a Snickers bar, a bag of potato chips, a can of Coke, and a blister pack containing two ChapSticks.

"You sure that's all you want?"

She'd grown quiet. "Yeah, I'm good."

"You know," he raised his voice, making sure the snob of a clerk heard him, "the airport might not find your luggage till tomorrow. You might as well pick out a change of clothes now, instead of having to come back down here later."

Sally turned her back to the clerk, and whispered, "Are you sure?"

He smiled. "Yeah, I'm sure."

She chose khakis and a sweater, and was making her way back to the register when she paused at a rack of swimsuits. She touched one, then sighed and started to walk away.

Jeff approached her. "You like to swim?"

"Love to. Used to, anyway."

He turned to the clerk. "What are your pool hours?"

"It closes at eleven."

Jeff tilted his head toward the rack of tropical-colored snippets of fabric. "Pick one."

Sally smiled wide, the first genuine smile he'd seen on her. It gave him a glimpse of the beauty that had been squelched for so long.

While he paid for the items, Sally stepped into the lobby. The clerk bagged everything, and verified the signature on the credit card slip against the back of the card. Then, she said, "Do you try to play Richard Gere often?"

"Pardon me?"

"*Pretty Woman*? Applying movie principles doesn't work in real life, *particularly* with one like her."

Jeff felt no need to explain that his relationship with Sally was completely different from that of the characters in the film. Instead, he borrowed a line from the movie. "Do you work on commission?"

"I most certainly do not. I'm part-time. I just work here for something to do."

"Your situation's as sad as hers, then, isn't it?" He waggled the large shopping bag. "Except for tonight."

He left the clerk trying to close her dropped jaw. He hoped it would take her the rest of the night to get her nose back in the air where it had started.

He asked Sally if she needed him to see her to her room.

"I'm fine," she said. (Her expression said, "You're kidding, right?")

He asked whether she needed any other items from the gift shop.

"I'm fine." (More emphasis but with an "Are-you-insane?" stare.)

He asked whether she needed any cash.

"I'm fine!" (She smiled, shooed him away. Her eyes danced a "Thank you, thank you. Now get lost so I can enjoy my room.")

He told her good-bye, and left, basking in his philanthropic self.

TWENTY-THREE

❦

$\mathcal{O}$N WEDNESDAY MORNING, Jeff sorted mail, returned phone calls, made a particularly lucrative deal with Lee Dunbar for jack-o'-lanterns, jotted the codes that corresponded to the photos that Sheila had earlier E-mailed to Lee on a slip of paper, and grabbed it and the directions that he'd printed out for the last-minute trip.

He found Sheila in the kitchen.

"Sheila, Lee bought three of the jacks, and I promised her we'd overnight them since it's almost Halloween. Here's a list of the codes." He glanced at his watch and cursed.

"Today? But—"

"Hon, my day's packed to the rafters. I've gotta go, or I'm going to be late. Can't Greer help you with it?"

"I guess, but—"

"You're a doll." He kissed her quickly, and headed for the back door.

Sheila mentioned something about having a full day herself but he was on the fly and didn't give her time to elaborate. He'd gotten an E-mail announcing a last-minute sale of an estate—one of those scenarios where the vulturous relatives were waiting in the wings with an auctioneer on retainer and a flyer printed up with everything but the date (rubber stamps and half-grown offspring on hand to fill in that last pesky detail). Jeff hated the approach but he couldn't afford to cut off his nose to spite his face. The stuff would sell, no matter what approach the inheritors used.

❦

It was a bust.

He arrived two beats before an unconsidered relative of the dearly departed stepped in and proved beyond all doubt that those who had instigated the sale were in violation of the law. The old house was in county jurisdiction, and several sheriff's deputies spent the better part of three hours trying to break up the crowd and get them to go home. Pickers don't generally give up easily. Jeff hung back, watched the deputies, listened to conjecture, visited with pickers he recognized, and waited. Finally satisfied that the only exchange of money that day was going to be between bondsmen and court clerks, he left empty-handed and ticked off.

He grabbed a late lunch of barbecued ham steak and fries at a local café, then started toward home.

He fought the tenacious feeling that something was wrong, but he couldn't put a finger on what it was. After having spent half an hour getting past his irritation over the sale—rather, the lack of a sale—he settled down to reviewing his day.

Sheila. That was it. He'd taken advantage of her time, hadn't even told her what he was up to or where he was going. In retrospect, he recognized that she'd been busy, too. He reached into his jacket pocket for his cell phone. He would apologize now, and again when he got home.

The phone wasn't there. He'd been in such a hurry that he'd forgotten the phone. He smacked the steering wheel with his palm.

It took another half hour to drive home. He pulled up the driveway, and saw Chris Fleming's sedan practically parked on the steps leading up to the back door. Jeff drove around it, and parked the woodie near the carriage house. *Why would Fleming pull up to the house like that?* Panic gripped him, followed quickly by reason. If anything had happened to Sheila, Greer would've reached him on the cell—

You forgot the cell, remember? his inner voice interrupted.

He shot up the back stairs and burst into the kitchen.

Greer gasped, and dropped a small silver tray. Tiny quiches rolled across the floor. The butler's face turned red, and he quickly chased after them.

"Sorry, man," Jeff said. "I saw Fleming's car, and I thought—"

"Greer?" Sheila's voice was an urgent whisper as she rushed into the kitchen. "Jeff? What's going on?"

Jeff's mouth dropped. Sheila was wearing a . . . dress?

Jeff recovered. "What *is* going on?"

"If you hadn't been in such a hurry this morning, you might have remembered. I have *company.*"

"Sheila, I . . . I am so sorry. There was this sale, and . . ."

"You can give me your excuses later. I only came out here because of the clatter. And, what have you done to Greer?" She stooped, put an arm around the butler's shoulders. "Are you okay?"

"Yes, ma'am. I'm terribly sorry about this." They stood, and Greer took the quiches to the wastebasket.

"Nonsense, Greer," Jeff said. "It's my fault. I saw Fleming's car and I thought something had happened to Sheila."

She said, "Greer would've called you, in that event."

"I forgot my—"

"I don't want to hear it," she said, cutting him off. "Now, pull yourself together and come with me."

She led the way toward the parlor.

The visit that Sheila had been so excited about had completely and shamefully slipped Jeff's mind. He reached out and touched Sheila's back as they walked but she didn't stop, didn't respond.

She paused outside the parlor door, breathed, then walked in. "I'm sorry for the interruption," she said pleasantly. "Jeff had some trouble with the door."

Chris Fleming stood by the fireplace, talking on his cell phone.

The woman seated on the love seat said, "I hope everything's okay."

"Oh, yes," Sheila said, "everything's fine." She breathed again, then said, "Jeff, I'd like you to meet my friend, Diane Fleming. Diane, my husband, Jeff."

The woman looked like Jeff imagined Sheila might look in twenty or thirty years. They had the same slender build, the same shoulder-length hairstyle (Mrs. Fleming's was ash-blonde where Sheila's was golden), and the same sense of timeless style.

"It's such a pleasure." He walked over quickly and took her hand. She wore an aqua and ivory tweed jacket with fringed edges over an ivory wool skirt. Her brooch and earring set appeared to be vintage, and the aquamarine stones winked as she moved. Her most outstanding feature was her aqua eyes, and he gave her extra points for knowing how to play up her attributes.

"The pleasure is mine," she said as Jeff took her hand. To Sheila, she said, "You're right, my dear. He's adorable."

"*That's* a picture I needed, Mother," Chris Fleming said

as he shut the phone's cover. He held it up before slipping it into his pocket. "Sorry about this, Sheila."

"I understand."

"You don't have to leave, do you?"

"No, fortunately." Fleming walked over and shook Jeff's hand. "Good to see you without a suspect between us."

Jeff tried to read the detective's face, to determine whether he was joking. "We're on the same side, remember?"

"Play nice, boys," Diane said.

Sheila invited the men to fix plates for themselves and take them to the library, while she and Diane visited in the parlor.

"Thanks, hon," Jeff said, and passed a plate to the detective. Sheila had pulled out all the stops in anticipation of the visit: there were crumpets, three varieties of scones, lemon curd, cucumber sandwiches, egg-salad sandwiches, petit fours, cookies, several spreads, and miniature quiches. Jeff loved those quiches, but after the kitchen fiasco he knew better than to take from the few left in front of him.

The women settled themselves in the parlor, chatting as if the men had already left. Diane was animated, clearly enjoying the outing. Jeff felt a pang of sadness; he hoped Sheila would find that place again soon, that ability to venture out.

He led the way to his library, and was grateful to find that Greer had a substantial fire going. As the two men sat opposite each other in front of the massive fireplace, Jeff said, "The fire feels good. Weather's really taken a turn for the worse."

"Sure does, and it sure has. They're predicting freezing rain and snow before the end of the month."

"Are we talking about the same city? Seattle?"

Fleming sat his cup and saucer on the table at his right

elbow. "That's what they say. Could be, they're trying to stir things up, keep people on their toes."

"You'll have a lot of grumpy goblins on your hands if Halloween freezes over."

"You got that right. This town takes Halloween seriously."

"Stop by here while you're out patrolling. This year, Sheila and I will be Scott and Zelda."

"No joke?" Fleming grinned like he'd been let in on a delicious secret.

Jeff smeared a morsel of strawberry bread with strawberry-infused cream cheese and held it up. "Do you think I'd jeopardize my privilege to this kind of treat over one night in a costume?"

"Yeah, well, if there are costumes involved any time other than Halloween, I don't want to hear about it."

Jeff wasn't used to the detective being chummy, so he steered the conversation in a more comfortable direction. "Any new leads in the Brock murder investigation?"

"Discussing murder over crumpets," Fleming said as he dolloped clotted cream atop one of the round, spongy biscuits.

"Yeah, I'll bet that's one you wouldn't have predicted."

Fleming washed the delicacy down with tea, wiped his face with a starched linen napkin monogrammed with a *T*, and cleared his throat.

Jeff didn't let go easily. "What about the hotel angle? Any new developments?"

"Every hotel in town is on order to report any and all father-daughter–type pairs. We've followed every lead, and they've all cleared. Like I told Mrs. Appleby, the guy probably blew out of town.

"The thing I'm hung up on at the moment," Fleming continued, "is that we found no sales receipts for the last three months. There was a small amount of cash in the register—about two hundred dollars, barely enough to set up a decent cash drawer for business. At any rate, robbery wasn't the motive, unless they were after something specific."

"It *is* an antiques shop. They might have been after a particular item."

"I'll give you that. Still, what about receipts? Even *you* keep receipts of transactions, right? She had nothing. We've gone through everything we know to go through."

Jeff thought about the files he and Lanny had found in the hidden cubby behind the janitor's closet.

As if Fleming had read his mind, he said, "Have you spoken with Smith lately?"

"Not in a few days, why?"

"I might be chummy over crumpets now but I won't be if your friend skips bail."

"I wouldn't expect you to be." Jeff struggled for a good grip on the dainty handle of the teacup, and the image put him in mind of a similar scene with Kevin Costner in *Open Range*. He got the delicate cup to his lips and sipped some tea. "I'll hook up with Lanny tomorrow and see if I can shake any info from him."

"You do that—" Fleming's cell phone rang over the last word. As he reached for it, Jeff said, "I'll get a warm-up, give you some privacy." He walked out of the library, and tapped on the parlor's entrance before entering. The ladies were deeply engaged in conversation, and Jeff hated to interrupt. He started to turn away but Sheila spotted him.

"Everything okay, hon? More tea?"

"Sure. Fleming, er, Chris," he said, nodding to Mrs. Fleming, "is taking a phone call."

The detective's mother shook her head. "That poor man never rests. I worry."

"He's a good detective," Jeff said.

"Yes. He learned from the best." She stared at a spot on her plate, then rattled her head slightly and addressed Jeff directly. "His father was chief in a college town. Killed in the line of duty five years ago."

"Oh, Diane, I'm so sorry," Sheila said.

"My condolences, Mrs. Fleming," Jeff added.

"Thank you, both of you." She smiled a smile that said she appreciated the sentiment, and that she'd heard it many, many times.

Fleming appeared in the doorway. "Mother, I'm not sure what to do with you."

"I've felt the same way about you many times, son." She grinned.

He quick-smiled, then became serious. "There's an emergency downtown, and I don't really have time to take you home."

Jeff said, "I'll be happy to drive you."

Sheila turned to Diane. "Can't you stay for dinner? Chris could come back when he's through, couldn't you, Chris?"

Fleming said, "That might—"

"I couldn't possibly impose," Diane interrupted.

"Nonsense," Jeff said. "I mean, I'll take you home now, if that's what you prefer, but I'm sure Sheila would love the opportunity to spoil you with more of her cooking."

"She *is* amazing," Diane said.

Sheila smiled. "Please say yes."

"Say yes, Mother, if you don't mind. Talbot won't be able to drive you home because he has to go with me."

Jeff stiffened. "Why do I have to go?"

"Because a girl's dead in a hotel room. A room you paid for."

TWENTY-FOUR
❦

*T*HE LOBBY OF the hotel looked like a convention for the Fraternal Order of Police. Fleming grasped Jeff's bicep, and ushered him along as they broke through the knots of uniformed cops.

Jeff had been so stunned during the ride down that Fleming had kindly kept talk to a minimum. Jeff knew that the detective wanted the story, *needed* the story, but first Jeff had to see for himself who was in the room. Till then, he couldn't accept what Fleming had said.

An elevator door slid open. Fleming guided Jeff inside, propped him against the brass rail, and punched *14*.

"It's not fourteen, you know." His voice sounded foreign to him.

Fleming took the notepad from his pocket with a single, economical sweep.

Jeff stared at the numbered keypad. He wanted to knock

that notepad out of Fleming's hand but he couldn't seem to get his arms to respond to his brain's commands. His arms were too heavy, as if he were standing at the bottom of a pool. "Your note will say it's fourteen but it's not. It's really thirteen."

"Don't think about that, Talbot," Fleming said. "You need to hold it together."

"I wasn't homeschooled but I learned to count before kindergarten." He tried to think. "Does that mean I *was* homeschooled? Either way, fourteen doesn't follow twelve."

"Here, it does."

"Don't you see? Sally wouldn't have stayed on the thirteenth floor."

"Didn't you come up to the room with her yesterday?"

"What are you trying to say? No. It wasn't about that. It wasn't anything like that."

"What was it like?"

"Just trying to give the girl a break. A donation. She impressed me."

He wondered if the numbering system had crossed her mind. If it *had* spooked her, she would have talked to someone at the desk about putting her on a different floor. Unless she'd been too excited about her reprieve from the street to think about such things.

He held out hope that it wasn't her in the room on the thirteenth floor. "People do things," he said, "like give up a seat on an airplane, then learn later that it went down. Or get mad over a late start for a road trip, then drive up on the scene of an accident on their route. Or realize they've been given a room on the thirteenth floor, and check out. Not check out, that's not what I meant. Check *with*. Check with the front desk, have them move you to a different room."

Fleming sighed, squeezed Jeff's shoulder.

"Did you check with the front desk?" Jeff asked.

"I checked."

"Maybe Sally didn't want to mess with a snooty desk clerk, so she found someone on her own, someone who would trade rooms with her. She's sharp. Smart." Jeff sighed. "She just needed another chance." Jeff knew his notions were far-fetched. But he'd witnessed scenarios more bizarre than those he'd described.

By the time he and Fleming stepped from the elevator, Jeff had built up a strong shield of hope.

Fleming turned left, and Jeff followed him to the end of the corridor. There, cops in uniform, investigators in dark suits, ME staff in white coats, and crime scene staff in street clothes all milled about from the hallway to the room.

Fleming parted the sea and stepped into the room. He glanced into the closet just inside the door, then looked at Jeff sympathetically.

Jeff tried to brace himself as he peeked inside the closet. A camel coat. He'd seen a camel coat at Fiona's, hadn't he? Or, had a camel coat been bought from Fiona's? He tried to remember, as his brain superimposed an image of the closet at Fiona's shop, and the broom handles crashed down on him. His shield took its first hit.

He saw a ChapStick on the nightstand. *Crash. Another hit.* The two magazines he'd bought the day before were on the bed. *And, another.* He wrapped his arms around himself, as if he might protect the dented armor from further abuse.

Under the window, a table held a large round tray of plates covered with metal hoods, a stemmed water glass marked with rivulets of condensation, and a bud vase with a pink rose that stooped over as if it were studying something of interest on the tray.

On the far side of the unmade bed, Fleming squatted on his haunches. After a moment, he stood and said, "Okay."

Jeff had to know. He willed himself to walk over.

Sally wore the top and khakis that he had purchased for her the afternoon before. Her worn-out tennis shoes were by the wall. In her right hand was a busted roll of pennies, and pennies were flung across the carpet.

"Old trick," said Fleming, pointing out a couple of the copper discs leaning against the baseboard next to the nightstand. "Packs a punch almost like brass knuckles. If she made contact, her killer's wearing one hell of a bruise."

Fleming turned away and asked what time the tray was delivered. Someone called out that it had been eleven-forty.

Jeff stared at the pennies. If she'd been able to afford quarters, would it have made a difference? His pulse pounded in his ears. The irony hit him: Here lay a woman who had survived everything that life on the streets had to offer, had survived it for years. Then, despite all her contingency plans, she was killed in one of Seattle's finest hotels. He wondered if that same thought had been her last one.

"Talbot."

Jeff jerked, looked at Fleming. "Huh?"

"Come with me." Fleming led him out of the room and down to the bank of elevators.

"You're in the deep, man," the detective said, pulling him aside. "I need you to pull it together, to deal with this."

Jeff slumped against the wall, shook his head. "I put her here. I'm responsible."

"You've been on enough cases to know that it doesn't work that way."

"I *don't* know anymore." Jeff closed his eyes, and a picture of her on the floor haunted him. He rubbed at his eyelids, trying to smudge the image. "She was . . . she had so much potential. It's such a waste."

"Then help her."

Jeff clenched his jaw. "Nothing's going to *help* her, Detective."

"I believe justice will, in a way. She would want us to

get the animal who did this. *Us*. You're with me on a case, you got it?"

"But I'm not—"

"You're not an agent anymore, we both know that. But you need to put your mind back there. If you can do it, it'll carry you through this, okay?"

Jeff shook his head. "I don't know how."

"The Bureau has to prep agents for this sort of thing, doesn't it? The ritual?"

"The ritual." It was coming back to him. "The repetitive steps you go through to enter a bad crime scene."

"Right. Have you ever done that?"

"Once or twice. It's been a long time."

"Go back there, find what you did to put your mind in that other place, that protective zone, and do it for this."

Jeff nodded.

Fleming patted him on the back a couple of times. "Come in and find me when you're ready." Fleming walked away.

Jeff got in the elevator and rode down.

He stood alone in the elevator bay on the ground floor, crawled into himself, and allowed a montage of his years as an agent to stream through his mind. He processed thoughts, images, recognized a constant.

He took a deep breath, and retrieved his cell phone.

When his party answered, Jeff said, "It's the old days, Gordy."

"Ah, the old days," said Gordy Easthope, Jeff's mentor, partner, friend. "Talbot, there's nothing new under the sun."

"That's right, isn't it?"

"That's right." Gordy cleared his throat. "Look, Talbot, I'll get your report later. Meanwhile, you know the drill."

"Right. The drill." Jeff closed the phone and put it away.

He pulled his wallet from his hip pocket, read all the words on the pasteboard ID. He rubbed his thumb over the old badge. That badge had a lot of dings on it. He couldn't feel them but he knew they were there. The ones from tonight weren't there; he had taken those hits himself. He had taken it personally. Now, he must put his badge back in front.

"The Feds are on this one, huh?"

Jeff looked up. It was Holcomb, the young officer he'd first met at Fiona's shop.

"Talbot, right?"

"You have a good memory."

Holcomb pushed a button on the panel, and stepped back.

Jeff waited, stared at his reflection in the doors. He remembered watching a tall, blonde woman poised in front of this door just yesterday. She had studied her reflection, smoothed her hair, pinched her cheeks for color. When the doors parted, she'd turned and smiled at him. She was happy. *That* was the image he would carry. He would remember the smile.

The doors in front of him slid open. "You coming up?"

Jeff nodded, followed Holcomb inside. The door closed, and Jeff punched *14*.

TWENTY-FIVE

❧

*I*N THE ROOM, Fleming was demonstrating a theory. "There are countless ways to commit a crime in a hotel room. My preliminary findings tell me that this one hinged on timing. Someone was either watching this room, or heard the vic mention ordering room service. When the waiter showed up with the tray, he was required to do this"—Fleming flipped the eye-level brass security latch—"so the door wouldn't close completely.

"Don't let them kid you," he added. "That's to protect themselves as much as anything else. Now, remember, it's a pneumatic door. In that slim window of time, while the guest showed the waiter to the table in the far corner of the room, our perp slipped through the door and stepped into the closet."

The group nodded collectively.

Fleming said, "Did everyone get the stats on the Brock murder?"

More nods.

"Let's find the link." Fleming turned.

By way of greeting, Jeff nodded once.

"Talbot, good to see you're back. Holcomb?"

"Yes, sir?"

"How are the conference rooms coming along?"

"The hotel's working out the details."

"Stay on them. I'll be down in a few."

He nodded. "Yes, sir." Another nod, this one to Jeff. "Talbot."

Jeff drifted toward the bathroom and peered inside.

Strewn everywhere were the contents from the fanny pack that he'd been privy to the day before in the restaurant. All of it had been dissected, as if someone were practicing a biology assignment. The aspirin tin was open, its rust-colored tablets spilled across the small counter; the flashlight's housing lay separate from the business end, and the batteries were in the sink; even the tampons' mechanisms were disassembled.

Hanging over the shower curtain rod was a tropical print swimsuit. He spotted a couple of pennies on the floor, another in the tub.

A woman squeezed past him, swept the room with her gaze, then set about labeling baggies.

Fleming joined them. "I don't know what he was looking for but he thought of hiding places that we snickered at back in training, before we learned it wasn't a joke."

The crime scene tech retrieved each item, secured it in its own baggie, and double-checked her labels as she went along. "I worked a case once where a killer had hidden a syringe in one of these little pink tubes," she said. "Turned out, it had the same poison in it that he'd used to kill his boss. Guess he thought no one would be gutsy enough to dig one of these out of a bathroom trash can and examine it.

"The corpses tell us a lot," she concluded, "but most of the rest we learn from the sick minds of the perps."

Jeff said, "And, they don't even know we have little mind games of our own." He exchanged a look with Fleming, went back to the corridor.

Fleming followed. "Let's go downstairs."

⌣⌣⌣

They sat in a corner in the hotel's open lounge area, out of earshot of the other patrons. There, Jeff filled the detective in on his pursuit of Sally, what she'd told him, the challenge she'd presented that led to the free night in a hotel. He told about her spunk, her wit, her past. Then he remembered the key. "Her shoe. There's a key in the pocket of her left shoe. She'd started to tell me what it fits when we were interrupted at the restaurant . . . something about what to do if anything happened to her." Jeff finished off his cup of coffee.

"Probably next of kin, somebody back home to contact. *If* we can find what it goes to." Fleming wrote in his notebook as he spoke. "Too many of the homeless leave us with nothing to go on. At any rate, it's a good sign, meant that she never gave up hope."

A commotion broke out in the lobby. On first glance, it looked like a hockey game—lots of shoving, body slamming, and elbowing—then Jeff sorted it out: Five beat cops were detaining Lanny and Tom Walcher. Barely. Fleming and Jeff bolted for the lobby.

"Jeff!" Lanny tried to jerk free. The cops looked imploringly at Fleming, who nodded, indicating they could release the men.

"Is it true? Is Sally—"

"She put up a real fight. She was tough."

Lanny slammed his palm against a marble column, then crumpled against it.

Walcher stuck his hands in his back pockets and paced. "She would've been better off on the streets."

Jeff said, "Try to remember it this way: She went out in a style she was once accustomed to."

Tom stopped pacing. "You're right. She had a wild ride."

Jeff stooped beside Lanny, told him how sorry he was. Lanny nodded.

"She had a key," Fleming said. "Either of you know—?"

"It's a metal document box," Walcher said. "A small one. Let me know when you want it, and I'll go back over to the Morrison and get it."

"Did she have an apartment at the Morrison?"

Walcher said, "Uh-uh, couldn't get her to commit to one. Anywhere. It's a long story."

Another disturbance broke out. Jeff stood, and stepped to one side in order to see what was going on. This time, a couple dressed in evening attire had tried to sneak out of the building. Two officers—one a hulk and the other a female—detained them.

"Detective, *please.*" The middle-aged man who addressed Fleming wore a dark green suit. The particular shade of green washed out his already pale complexion and gave his brown hair an ashy quality. The hotel name badge pinned to his suit lapel identified him as General Manager Daniels. He grinned nervously. "Those people clearly aren't murderers. If you'll just allow us to—"

"No one leaves without giving a statement and stats."

"And, when will you have someone seeing to that?"

Fleming spoke with a clenched jaw. "When your assistant manager lets us know which rooms are available for us to conduct the interviews in."

Daniels tilted his head and touched two fingers to his left temple, as if the word "assistant" had lodged there. He straightened. "I'll check into that. Meanwhile, what am I supposed to do about my guests who have tickets for the theater?"

Fleming glared at him. "Haven't you heard, Mr. Daniels? Murder trumps Mozart."

"Sounds like a title," Jeff said.

"It's been done." This was from Walcher. "They called it *Amadeus*. Salieri was the bad guy."

Fleming stared at Walcher for a second.

A female wearing a navy blue blazer and black skirt approached, heels clicking on the marble floor. "Mr. Daniels, upper management's on the phone again."

Daniels sighed wearily and followed the woman back toward the registration desk. Jeff suspected those conference rooms would free up any second.

Fleming looked from Walcher to Lanny. "When was the last time either of you talked to Sally?"

Jeff held out his hand to Lanny, helped him up off the floor.

Walcher said, "She called the Morrison a little before noon today, and talked to both of us. Lanny was there helping move furniture out of apartments for the carpenters. She said that Wash had arranged with housekeeping for her to have a couple extra hours in the room."

"Who's Wash?" Fleming asked.

"He's a bellman here. Sally was going to meet him for a late-afternoon drink when his shift was over."

Fleming flagged down Holcomb. "Find the guy they call Wash. He's where we begin."

⟨⟨⟨⟩⟩⟩

When Holcomb returned, he said, "Two rooms are set up at the end of the north corridor on the mezzanine. Your first subject is already up there."

"Good," said Fleming. "Grab some help and start moving everyone else in that direction."

The press of people in the wide corridor outside the conference room put Jeff in mind of a cattle car. To the credit of the Seattle PD, guests and hotel employees alike were processed quickly despite protests, accusations, and threats of lawsuit.

The official names of the two rooms opposite each other had been covered with sheets of paper on which someone had printed in block letters, Interrogation Room, and Holding Room.

"Talbot," Detective Fleming said, "take Smith and Walcher to the holding room. I'll see all of you as quickly as possible."

Jeff, Lanny, and Tom walked through the double doors and into the large room. Four hotel staff members in white shirts and black trousers busily set up round tables and un-stacked towers of chairs. And complained about the inconvenience. At a long table on the south wall, two female employees set up a beverage station. Jeff wondered how long it would be before the huge, cylindrical coffeemakers would finish percolating.

He stationed himself at the table with the best view of the exit, hoping that the doors would remain open. He wanted to monitor activity in the wide corridor. Lanny and Tom joined him, and the trio sat in silence.

Jeff studied the faces and mannerisms of the others in the room, rearranged himself on the chair, glanced at the coffee urns, tried not to fidget, and generally watched time pass. He glanced at his watch. Fleming and Wash had been in the interrogation room for only seven minutes. It seemed like thirty.

Jeff was about to check the coffee when the door of the interrogation room swung open and Fleming stepped into the corridor. He buttonholed Holcomb, said something, and Holcomb took off.

Fleming stepped to the holding room door. "Walcher, come with me."

A young, clean-cut Latino man in a bellman's uniform exited interrogation as Fleming and Walcher entered. The bellman walked into the holding room and pulled up a chair at Jeff's table.

"Hey, Lanny," he said.

"Hey, Wash. Jeff, this is Washington Ruiz."

Jeff shook the man's extended hand. He struck Jeff as someone at ease with corporate presidents and the homeless alike.

"This business with Sally's a bad trip, man," Wash said with only a hint of a Latino accent. He loosened his tie and unbuttoned the neck of his shirt.

"Yeah," Lanny said. "You two were gonna get together when you got off work?"

"Didn't happen. She was a no-show downstairs, so I tried her phone and got no answer. Couldn't get her to come to the door, either. I got one of the gals from housekeeping to open her door."

"What time was that?" Jeff asked.

"Around three-thirty. I got off work at three."

"Did you give them anything that might help them find Sally's killer?"

"Apparently so. The *management* in this place had orders from the cops to report any men checking in here with their daughters."

Jeff sat forward. "You're saying a guy checked in with his daughter, and they didn't report it?"

"I'm sayin', management didn't tell us lowly peons who do all the work around here about it. Turns out, the guy lied when he checked in, told the clerks he was alone. People try to get by with that all the time. Cheapskates." Wash grunted. "But this one, he had a kid with him. One of the housekeepers told me."

Jeff deduced that Fleming had sent Holcomb to track down the man's billing record.

He'd started to say something when Fleming bolted from the interrogation room while shouting something on a walkie-talkie.

"Wait here," Jeff told Lanny, and took off after the detective.

He caught up with him at the elevators. "You can come up," Fleming warned, "but you'll have to stay back."

Jeff nodded.

On the ride up, Fleming said, "There's more to Walcher's conversation with Sally. She told him a guest had asked if she'd watch his daughter—said he needed to leave but the kid was having too good of a time in the pool. They had met earlier in the elevator on the way down."

"So, they were on the same floor?"

"Yeah. Walcher said that she told the guy she couldn't take responsibility for a stranger's kid."

"What happened then?"

"From what she told Walcher, the guy was irritated. He left the pool and took the girl with him. Sally apparently went up to her room after another half hour or so, ordered room service, and called Walcher while she waited for it to arrive."

"So, you're going to search the room he checked out of? After housekeeping's been in?"

"I'll do you one crazier: He's still registered."

Jeff let that sink in. He followed Fleming down the corridor toward what had been Sally's room. Four officers stood at the adjoining door, guns at the ready. Clearly, Fleming had put wheels in motion from downstairs.

Fleming rapped on the door with his fist, all but knocking it off its hinges. When he got no answer, he ripped the small Do Not Disturb placard from the key slot and inserted a card. He drew his weapon, gave a nod to the cops, and threw open the door.

Jeff patted under his left arm, and, realizing that he no longer carried a weapon, hung back.

A dozen seconds passed, then the officers walked out of the room. One of them stepped inside Sally's room, and presently the female tech who had been bagging Sally's items joined Fleming.

Jeff eased up to the door, and glanced inside.

Fleming saw him, and said, "It's empty, no personal belongings."

"But . . ." Jeff stopped.

"Just because you pay for a room . . ." Fleming started.

Jeff finished with, "Doesn't mean you sleep there."

Fleming retrieved the walkie-talkie clipped on his belt, and said into it, "Levin?"

"Yeah?" the box squawked.

"Use that info you're tracking, put out an APB. And include Canada."

"Detective?" The female tech came to the doorway with a sheet of paper in her latex-gloved hands.

"Don't touch," she said, holding it up for them to see.

Jeff leaned in. The lined notebook paper was filled with penciled words written in a small, tight cursive. Block letters above the body of text read: MAJOLICA. In the upper right-hand corner was the name Allison.

TWENTY-SIX

ON THE WAY back to the mezzanine, Fleming said, "We've run out of time for games. What were you really doing that day in Fiona Brock's antiques shop?"

Jeff said, "This'll go quicker if Lanny's in on the answer."

They found Lanny and Tom where Jeff had left them.

Fleming said, "Walcher, Holcomb's going to give you a lift to the Morrison in order to get Sally's lockbox."

"Yes, sir," Walcher said.

"Smith," Fleming said, "come with us."

In the interrogation room, Fleming gave instructions to Holcomb, then motioned Lanny and Jeff to sit opposite him at a rectangular table.

After they'd seated themselves, Jeff said, "Lanny, we have to tell Fleming everything."

Lanny stared at Jeff before turning his attention to Fleming. "Some of it doesn't seem very important."

"Smith, two people are dead. All of it's important. Everything becomes a potential clue.

"Evidence links a man and his daughter to Brock's shop and this hotel," Fleming continued, "where they had contact with Sally. As far as we can determine, they've been in Seattle since the night before Brock's murder. Majolica seems to be the common denominator."

Lanny's gaze darted from Fleming to Jeff and back again. "My wife died last month."

"What?" Jeff wasn't sure he'd heard right.

"My condolences," Fleming said. "I wasn't aware you were married."

Jeff said, "When did you find out that Janet had died?"

"I couldn't take the suspense anymore, so I took a chance and called her family out east. I said I was an old friend from school. Whoever answered the phone said that Janet had passed away last month. I was so shocked I didn't say anything. The other person didn't, either, at first. Then she said she was sorry, and hung up."

Lanny looked to Jeff, who began filling in the blanks for Fleming. "Their marriage was annulled several years ago, against their wishes. They were underage. The majolica figurine belonged to Lanny's family. He'd given it to his bride, Janet, as a wedding gift."

"It had unique markings," Lanny said. "When Fiona showed it to me, I knew without a doubt that it was the same one. And, I knew that something must be wrong."

Fleming said, "Have you been hiding out?"

"No." He glanced furtively at Jeff. "Talbot might think so. He's had a hard time keeping tabs on me. But I've stayed in town. When I haven't been busy making a living, or taking care of things I do for other tenants at the Morrison, I've been going to every antiques shop and flea market I could find, trying to locate that figurine."

Fleming seemed deep in thought. "Have you been watching your back?"

"No."

"Have you been told to meet anyone, then you arrived and no one showed?"

"No, nothing like that."

Fleming thought some more. "Maybe it's a set-up, and somebody used the majolica to find you."

"But I haven't been hiding," Lanny protested.

"I had considered that, too," Jeff said. "But how'd they get *that* particular piece?"

Fleming said, "Maybe her family has already dispersed her stuff."

"Already?" Lanny looked stricken. "That's cold."

Fleming exhaled. "Some do it quick, cold turkey, like drug rehab. Others never do. You'll have to ask the shrinks which way is better."

"It's all one heck of a coincidence," said Jeff.

"Which leads us back to a set-up."

"Why would anyone want to set up Lanny?"

"What about it, Smith? Any ideas?"

"I don't have anything," Lanny replied.

Jeff said, "You know, it just hit me. What if you're in line to inherit something from *your* family? You told me you were from money. Maybe it's not about Janet at all."

"That never crossed my mind," Lanny said. "But it doesn't matter if it's true. I don't want anything from them."

Fleming sat back. "Good theory, Talbot, but it doesn't scan. Smith's family forced his wife out of the picture. It's not logical that they would find her in order to locate him."

"What's worse is she's gone now, so I can't ask her about any of it." Lanny rubbed at a scratch in the tabletop. He might have been evaluating it for renovation and resale, but Jeff knew that was the furthest thing from his mind.

"That must be hard to take."

"It was. Is. I mean, I just found out. It opened up old wounds."

Fleming made notes. "Didn't you try to find her when you were legally of age?"

"For awhile. But I was young. I didn't have any money."

Fleming said, "You're still young. Twenty-six?"

"And I still don't have any money." He shook himself. "Like I already said," he went on, "I knew when the majolica surfaced it meant something had happened to Janet. After I found out for sure, I went back to searching for the figurine. Don't ask me to try to explain it, because I can't. But I have to have that majolica. It's all I've got, you know?"

An alarm sounded in Jeff's head. "I just remembered. Sally told me yesterday that she went back to Fiona's shop after the fight."

"Sally did?" Lanny said. "Why?"

"To confront her about reneging on your deal."

Fleming said, "What time?"

"I don't know. She said a customer came in and Fiona told Sally to get lost. She also said Fiona had called him 'a *real* customer.'"

Fleming said, "Sally saw the fight between you and Brock, went back later, probably right before you found Brock, and saw a guy who entered the shop." Fleming thought. "Mustang Sally saw the killer. What's worse, she probably didn't even realize it."

Jeff frowned. "So, you think he stayed in town all this time to find her?"

"It would seem so." Fleming stood, circled the table. "I wonder if the 'real' customer was a customer at all?"

"He was real, all right," Lanny said, "if he's the one who paid Fiona all that cash."

Something Jeff recognized as guilt hit his gut like a rock. *The secret closet.*

"What cash?" Fleming said.

Jeff and Lanny exchanged a look.

Fleming slammed his notepad on the table. "I *knew* it. You took her files that day, didn't you?"

"Not intentionally." Jeff told all of it then: how they'd

nosed around for a murder weapon, how they'd gotten Fiona's cat from Meredith at the coffeehouse next door, and how Lanny had shown him the secret cubbyhole behind the mop buckets.

"Lanny was about to show me what was in the files when we heard the front door," Jeff concluded.

Fleming glared at them. "Where are they?"

Lanny said, "In my apartment."

"Intact?"

"Yes, sir, all of it. Even the cash."

"How much cash?"

Lanny paused. "Thirty-five hundred."

"Does Walcher have a key to your apartment?"

Lanny shot out of his chair. "You can't—"

"Lanny," Jeff said, "the faster they can inspect it, the faster they can catch up with this guy. Believe me, this way's better than a team of detectives ripping your place apart."

Lanny sat back down, signaling defeat.

Fleming punched buttons on his cell phone. "Holcomb, where are you? Good, put him on the phone. Walcher? Fleming. Smith's about to give you instructions. Do what he says, give the items to Holcomb." Fleming handed the cell phone to Lanny, who revealed the location of the files.

When that was done, Fleming said, "Let's go antiquing."

☜☞

Jeff suspected that tonight's scene at Garden Gate Antiques was much like the one after Fiona's body had been found.

Somewhere along the way, Fleming had arranged for the female crime scene tech to meet them. She had apparently picked up the key to the back door on her way over, because she was standing by Fiona's desk when they arrived. Either that, Jeff thought, or she moonlighted as a lock pick.

Holcomb was there, too, bogarting the accordion file in one arm and a locked metal box about eight inches square and four inches deep in the other.

The rest of Sally's story, Jeff thought.

"Gwen," Fleming said, handing a tiny key to the tech, "this should fit the box. It belonged to tonight's vic."

Jeff was glad finally to have a name to associate with the woman.

Fleming turned to Lanny. "The closet?"

Lanny cracked open the door apprehensively. Jeff figured he was anticipating the clatter of broom handles. But when nothing jumped out at him, he opened the door fully, then shoved things out of the way to reveal the hidden panel. He popped it open, found the light switch, and stepped aside.

The contents of the closet appeared to be exactly as Jeff and Lanny had left them over two weeks earlier. Brown paper grocery bags and coated-paper shopping bags were piled and crammed into every conceivable space on top of lidded boxes and warped cartons.

Fleming surveyed the mess, shook his head, then shucked his overcoat and suit jacket. After finding a wall hook on which to hang them, he moved in and started retrieving bags.

Gwen joined them, reported that there was nothing unusual in the small box, then set up shop by placing her fingerprint kit on an upturned bucket. She snapped on a fresh pair of latex gloves and emptied the bags of their contents as they came at her.

A time or two during the process, Lanny asked the pair to be careful, citing the possibility of treasures among the junk. After a while, Lanny and Jeff cleared some space and sat on the floor with their backs against the wall.

Holcomb roamed, checking in every now and then, and raising his brows in astonishment before drifting away.

"That's it!" Lanny said.

Gwen had unearthed a celestial globe from a wrap of old newspaper. Jeff gave her credit for smarts: She held the edges of the metal band with her fingertips.

"It, what?" Fleming said.

"That globe! The guy who stood by the front door when Fiona and I argued. He picked it up."

Gwen nodded without comment and went to work lifting prints. Fleming continued pulling plunder from the cubby.

Jeff surveyed the broom closet. All manner of statuettes and what-nots were crowded together on the floor, surrounded by wads of newsprint, sections of bubble wrap, and foam peanuts. It looked like the room Sheila had set up for packing and shipping eBay sales—if you'd fired a cannon into it.

Gwen finished with the globe and returned to unpacking.

Jeff was gazing out the door, wishing Fleming would send Holcomb for a round of coffee, when he heard something like a quiet gasp next to him. He turned, saw Lanny's trembling hands reach for Gwen's treasure.

"Uh-uh," she said, holding it out of reach. "Prints."

Lanny pulled back, and Jeff saw how much effort it took.

Jeff recognized the majolica figurine from the description he'd been given. The farmer was weathered, raw-boned, stoop-shouldered from the burden of a weight he was assigned to carry forever. He looked amazingly like Lanny.

Lanny found his voice. "The original provenance is in those files. You'll find my name on it, and my date of birth. The least you can do is let me hold it."

"Give me just a moment to check it," Gwen said, not without compassion.

"I gave Sally a photocopy to hold for me."

Gwen said, "The only things in the box are a few photos and keepsakes, an old Iowa driver's license, and a contact for emergencies."

Lanny said, "It wouldn't be in the box. Sally wrapped it around the batteries in her flashlight."

Jeff caught the look exchanged between Fleming and Gwen. To Lanny, he said, "Didn't you hold the figurine when Fiona first showed it to you?"

"She wouldn't show me the actual piece," Lanny confessed. "Only pictures."

Gwen finished lifting prints, and sought a nod of approval from Fleming before placing the figurine in Lanny's hands.

Lanny gripped the figurine, caressed it, looked it all over, touched the letters painted under each basket. At length, he held it against his chest. He closed his eyes, and propped his chin on the farmer's straw hat.

Jeff suspected that Lanny had at last found closure.

If there had been any doubt in Jeff's mind about Lanny's innocence, what he had just witnessed erased it. He would not have killed Fiona, who had been his only link to this moment.

Jeff stood, and with a discreet tilt of his head asked the investigators to join him in the other room.

Once there, Fleming said, "So, Sally's killer has the copy of the provenance."

Gwen said, "Does it make sense that someone would stay in town killing people, just to get a *copy?* What good can it do him without the actual antique?"

"Maybe he thinks he can use it as proof of ownership if the figurine surfaces."

"Which it did," Jeff said. "But why here?"

"Insurance." Fleming wiped his brow on his sleeve. "Usually means *you* think that *they* think that you know something."

"In other words," Holcomb said, "you know you're in danger."

Fleming said, "Or that you're in on something you shouldn't be. Which also means you're in danger."

Jeff said, "Looks like Fiona had some kind of scam going. That would explain the cash in the accordion file, wouldn't it? A payoff."

"Well, whatever it was, she left some interesting clues to her own murder."

⌘

Jeff rolled home just before midnight, vaguely remembering Diane Fleming and wondering whether she'd been put up in one of the guest rooms.

Sheila looked up from the book she was reading, waited. She didn't speak.

He went to her. "Sweetheart, I want to say again that I'm sorry. I completely forgot about your plans with Fleming's mother today when I insisted that the stuff be shipped to Lee."

Sheila said, "No, I offered to handle all the shipping in our joint venture, and you don't have to worry: Lee Dunbar will have her jack-o'-lanterns in hand tomorrow before you start on your first cup of coffee. Also, I don't expect you to cater to my social life. I'm not sure *how* my husband could let such a momentous occasion as Diane's first visit to our home slip his mind, but I suppose my husband's not as interested in my life as somebody else's! It would've been nice, though, if you'd told me up front that you had a girl stashed in a hotel—a very nice hotel, at that."

"You're right. I should've told you about that."

"Are you hiding something?"

"Not anymore."

"What's that supposed to mean?"

"Huh?" Jeff rubbed his forehead. "Oh, nothing to do with the girl. I was thinking about something that Lanny and I hadn't shared with Fleming. That's why I was so late tonight. We took the detective to Fiona Brock's shop. Turns out there was a lot of evidence there, in a secret closet."

"Would you *please* tell one story at a time? And by the way, have you noticed that your messes always come in pairs?"

"Do you think I choose to have this stuff happen?"

"I really don't know. Maybe you do. Maybe you regret getting out of law enforcement. Is that it?"

"Shouldn't we keep our voices down, Sheila?"

"Why?" She raised the volume a couple notches, as if to say she would do as she pleased under her own roof.

"I assume Diane Fleming is in the guest room, since I left her son still working on the case."

"That's what you get for assuming. Chris called to tell

her it was going to be a long night, so Greer drove her home around eight. Didn't he tell you?"

Eight o'clock. Where were they at eight? He couldn't recall. "No, he didn't mention it."

"And you didn't even think of it."

"Sheila. A girl is dead."

"I know that, and I'm sorry. I really am. But it'll be interesting to hear you explain why you're buying two-hundred-dollar hotel rooms for girls off the street."

"It wasn't like that, and I think you know it."

"Do you know how difficult it was for me to hold myself together for an entire evening with Diane here, after her son blurted out that my husband had a dead girl stashed in a hotel room?"

Uh-oh. He had thought he'd learned to look at situations from everyone's point of view. "I . . . didn't think of it from that angle."

"No, you didn't. Why am I not surprised?"

"Sheila—"

"Fortunately, Diane had an arsenal of stories about being a cop's wife for thirty years. She filled a lot of dead air while I tried to get back on track. She said she learned from the get-go that nothing is as it seems, and that every cop's wife worth her salt realizes that."

Jeff smiled. "Smart lady."

"Yes, she is. And stop smiling."

Jeff knew his wife. She had to get all her pent-up emotions out in the air before she'd hear what he had to say. "I think my wife's that way, too," Jeff said. "She's just a little out of practice."

Sheila fought a smile.

"Now, let me tell you about a friend of Lanny's called Mustang Sally who I met only yesterday, and how her last night . . ." he paused, reined in his emotions, ". . . and how her last night was spent in a two-hundred-dollar hotel room instead of on the street."

TWENTY-SEVEN

❧

*S*HEILA CUT ONE-foot lengths of orange and black curling ribbon and knotted them around a cellophane neck before dragging the scissors blade down each one with a *zip*. She tossed the wrapped and decorated popcorn ball into the tissue-lined vintage laundry basket (Nantucket, circa early 1920s), and repeated the noosing process.

She and Greer had been popping corn all day, working methodically while pelting rain and *Hocus Pocus* served as mood-setting backdrops.

The butler sorted out the unpopped kernels while Sheila cooked up batches of corn syrup and orange Jell-O to make the tasty glue that would bind the popped corn together.

It was one of Sheila's Halloween traditions, making several dozen of her special orange popcorn balls with peanuts for the trick-or-treaters. The regulars knew to arrive at the Talbot house early if they wanted one of the limited-edition treats. If they missed out, they had to settle for store-bought candy.

"I'm excited that Halloween falls on a Friday," Sheila said. "It's always more fun to have the kids show up on the actual day. They're more in the spirit."

"So to speak," Jeff said as he sneaked a bite of the gooey concoction.

She slapped at him playfully.

"How many more batches do you have to make?"

"Oh, another three or four today, then we'll finish up in the morning. That'll leave plenty of time to get ready." She measured a portion of peanuts and poured it into her bubbling cauldron. "Have you made sure your costume fits?"

"It'll fit. What about yours?"

"Perfectly, thank you."

"I've got some reading to catch up on." Jeff freshened his cup of coffee. "I'll take the cordless with me to the conservatory and screen calls while you two finish this."

"Thanks, hon," Sheila called after him.

Jeff juggled a cup of coffee, the newspaper, and the cordless phone, and made his way out to the conservatory. He'd been watching the sky all morning, hoping for a break in the rain and the dreariness. Sometimes he liked the conservatory while it was raining, the *tap-tap* on the glass panes. It was almost like sitting under a shelter at a campsite. The only thing missing was the campfire. Even the birds were settled down for a change, napping, enjoying the lulling rhythm of the rain.

He finished the paper and was halfway through a lengthy article about Roycroft furniture when the phone rang.

Bargain Basement's eyes popped open and his feathers seemed to stand on end. "Get the phone!" He squawked. "Get the phone!"

"I'm getting the phone. Now keep quiet."

Second ring.

"Get the phone!"

Jeff hopped up and pulled the cage cover down. The bird protested and Jeff could've sworn the thing yelled, "Hey!"

"Hello?"

Lanny said, "It's me."

"Hi. How are you holding up?"

"Not good."

"I . . . I'm really sorry, Lanny."

"Thanks. For everything. Look, I've got a lead on something you've been wanting."

"Good. If it's that item for Sheila, go ahead and get it. I trust your judgment."

"I'd rather you see it."

Jeff had promised Sheila he'd help with some business stuff (his idea, in an attempt to assuage guilt over the previous day's preoccupation) in order to free up her time for the Halloween preparations. He said, "Is there any way around doing that today?"

Lanny's sigh was almost imperceptible over the phone line. Finally, he said, "Remember the vesta cases I found a few years back?"

It had been years since the vesta case but the code—one of several that FBI Jeff and Informant Lanny had cooked up—instantly put Jeff on the same page with Lanny. "I'm leaving now."

"Make sure no one tries to horn in on this deal."

Code: *Make sure you're not followed.* "That's a promise."

⌣⌣⌣

The vesta case had nothing to do with vesta cases—those early match containers that preceded the Zippo lighter. It was Jeff's pet name for an investigation he'd headed up to crack a cigarette smuggling ring that operated out of an abandoned warehouse near a West Seattle pier. Lanny's info had been key in Jeff's cracking the case, and since Lanny was a picker at the time and Jeff already knew a lot about antiques, they'd come up with the innocuous-sounding code.

To his advantage, Sheila was having too much fun preparing for the next day's festivities. All he had to say was that there was some sort of trouble, and that he'd be back as soon as he could.

He drove the Jimmy instead of the woodie, and spent an extra twenty minutes making sure no one was following him. It was a challenge: heavy rains made it hard enough to see the pavement, let alone a tail two or three cars back. Fortunately, it also meant that any would-be watchman would have the same trouble picking out the dark blue SUV.

Satisfied that he was alone, he crossed the West Seattle Bridge and looped a ribboned path on his way to the old warehouse.

He pulled up next to Lanny's old truck. Lanny hopped into the Jimmy.

The young man was as white as a ghost, and looked as if he hadn't slept in a month.

Jeff tightened his grip on the steering wheel. "Hit me with it."

"I think I found the murder weapon."

Jeff waited another beat, then exhaled and relaxed his hold. "That shouldn't be a problem. You didn't kill Fiona, therefore you didn't use a murder weapon."

"I picked it up without thinking. It's not your typical murder weapon, and I couldn't figure out what it was doing there."

"What *it?*"

"The mill pack."

"Mill pack? Do you mean *pick?*"

"No, pack. It's like a mallet with a row of thick steel blades embedded in it to roughen up the stones for grinding grain in grist mills."

"Sounds like a weapon, all right, but what makes you think it's the murder weapon?"

"You mean, besides the fact that the row of blades probably matches those lines on the back of Fiona's neck?

There's . . . stuff on it." Lanny shuddered. "I put it in a plastic bag to preserve the evidence."

Jeff dropped his head back against the headrest. "God, Lanny. Why didn't you just call Fleming?"

"You're kidding, right? This will convince him that I killed her."

No, but hiding it will. Think. Pros usually ditch the weapon quickly. "Lanny, lots of people pick up items without thinking. If it was in a Dumpster a block or so from her shop, or—"

"It was in the back of my pickup. I found it when I was rummaging through the junk in the bed to find my jack."

"Wait, your truck wasn't at Fiona's last night."

"No. Some good Samaritan had aired up the tire when I went back there for it that week. But it was flat again today."

"You found the mill pack inside the camper shell, right? I thought you kept that locked."

"Sure I do. But I'd unlocked it before going in to buy the majolica, so I wouldn't have to mess with the keys when I carried the boxes out. When I went to leave after the fight with Fiona, one of the tires was flat, and I was too mad to mess with it. I took off walking down the alley. I wasn't thinking about the unlocked shell."

"And when you returned you found the body."

"Yeah."

Jeff looked beyond Lanny, toward the old pickup. "Is it still in there?"

"No, I hid it at my apartment. I didn't want it in the truck when I was going to drive down here to meet you. What if I broke down or something? Next thing you know, a cop comes along and runs a check on me, it shows I'm still under suspicion for murder. How does it look if they find the weapon in my vehicle?"

"Almost as bad as finding it hidden in your home."

Lanny rubbed his face with shaking hands.

Jeff tried to contact Fleming but got his voice mail, and

left a message asking him to meet them at the Morrison as soon as possible.

He shut the cell phone. "He's probably on the line with someone else. If we don't hear from him by the time we reach your place, we'll try again."

"Is he going to believe me?"

"Lanny, you're not going to do anything stupid, are you?"

"You mean besides hiding the murder weapon? No. Truth is, I wasn't hiding it when I called you. I just . . . It shook me up, you know?"

"I do know."

"Your neck is still on the line for me, and I won't jeopardize that by skipping out. I gave you my word, and I'll stick by it."

"See you over there, then." Jeff watched as Lanny got out of the Jimmy, settled in his old truck, and pulled away.

⌘

End-of-day traffic mixed with heavy rain made for a fine happy-hour cocktail. Jeff tried a few circle-round maneuvers, and got hung up behind a fender-bender for his efforts. When he finally reached Tom's post at the Morrison, he was told that Lanny and the detective were already upstairs. Jeff rode the elevator up to the fifth floor, and thought that when all this was over, he was through with elevators for awhile. And murder, too, while he was at it.

They were almost ships passing in the night. As he stepped from one cage, he glimpsed Lanny with Fleming in another. Jeff caught the closing door as someone on the other side hit the button to hold it open. He entered the box, and realized it had to have been Fleming who'd held the door because Lanny's hands were cuffed behind his back.

"You *are* kidding, right?" Jeff said.

Fleming said, "One of you could've told me that Smith owned a pickup."

"You never asked."

"We learn from our mistakes. Smith and I have learned a lot today, haven't we, Smith?"

"I know *I* have," Lanny said.

Jeff said, "Come on. You know he didn't do this."

"You're raising a bigger stink than he did, Talbot. There are too many unanswered questions. And this latest development leaves me no choice."

"But—"

"Don't worry about it, Jeff," Lanny said. "I'm innocent."

"And, if he is," Fleming said, "he's a damned sight safer in lock-up."

⟳

Jeff gave Sheila a recap of what had happened.

When he'd finished, she said, "So, you're sure there's nothing we can do to help Lanny?"

"Not that I know of." Jeff rubbed a hand over his face. "Maybe Fleming's right. Jail might be the safest place for Lanny right now."

"Blanche hired some security, did you know that?"

"I haven't talked to her. I don't think she has to worry, but if it makes her feel better . . ." He shrugged.

"Do you think you're safe, Jeff? I mean, you've gotten pretty mixed up in this. Maybe you should have some security, too."

"You don't really believe that, do you? All I did was vouch for Lanny so he could get out of jail. Look at where that got him."

"Back in jail?"

"Short version, yeah. I'm not a threat, so there's no motive."

"I suppose you're right."

He rubbed his face. "I'm beat."

"Dinner will be ready soon. We can make it an early night, if you want."

"You've got a date."

~∞~

Jeff couldn't sleep. He'd been lying there awake for about half an hour, near as he could tell. That's how it usually went when he turned in too early.

He rolled from one side to the other, careful not to disturb Sheila, squinted at the clock's face till he made out the time: four-thirty.

He thought about stuff. He thought about life. He thought about the stuff of life, and how we all spend a lifetime amassing stuff, weeding out stuff, acquiring stuff, downsizing our stuff, downsizing our homes to control our bent toward amassing stuff.

He recalled the plaque by the door of Lanny's small, spare apartment, and the profound story it told: "If you have a rug on your floor, you have too much." Quite a statement for Lanny, who made his meager living acting as the conduit between people and stuff.

Jeff flipped back onto his other side. He thought about Sally, how she'd winnowed down *her* stuff to what might be contained comfortably on her own body.

He thought about how he'd convinced old man Hoffman that he didn't need all that stuff. Yet, look at his own home: a massive Victorian wedding cake of a structure, four stories, with a widow's walk besides, and so chock-full of stuff that . . . well, he didn't know what. All he knew was that he would be Hoffman in thirty years, a slave to stuff. Who was he kidding? He was Hoffman now. He paid Lucy and Polly. Greer, too, when you thought about it, to clean all his stuff. Although, Greer was mostly for Sheila, her link to Pike Place Market, the post office, the grocery store, the shops along Queen Anne Avenue, the downtown department stores.

Jeff sighed. Was he growing tired of his profession already? Or had the glimpse into Lanny's world been a dose of reality? Jeff didn't know, and suspected that even if he did, he wouldn't know what to do about it.

"You awake?" Sheila's voice, gritty.

"Did I wake you? I'm sorry."

"You okay?"

"Yeah, just thinking."

"What on earth about?"

"Just stuff." He sighed again, flipped over, thought about not thinking, and, finally, slept.

TWENTY-EIGHT

❧

$\mathcal{D}$ARKNESS DESCENDED UPON the hobgoblins of Halloween, and the Talbot household was ready.

Most of the autumn decorations had already been set up for Jeff's birthday, so he'd spent the afternoon sweeping the porches, replenishing leaves in old apple baskets on the steps and the front porch, and fluffing and stuffing scarecrows propped up against bales of straw under the trees. The past three weeks had whipped and beat the stuffing right out of the droopy characters. Jeff knew how they felt.

He and Sheila now stood in the foyer, looking as if they'd stepped out of *The Great Gatsby*. Sheila excitedly twirled her rope of pearls, then executed a quick-step circle, putting her flapper fringe into motion. The tall feather tucked into the back of the beaded band circling her head swayed slightly.

"Did you get that feather off one of your birds?" Jeff asked.

"Don't be silly." Sheila slapped him playfully.

He curled an arm around her shoulders and gave her a squeeze. "Just teasing."

"I'd kiss you but I don't want to take the chance of getting red on your white tuxedo shirt." She touched his face with her gloved hand, and for the hundredth time, peeked out the window beside the front door. "I'm so afraid someone's going to take Poe. I loved the notion of displaying him out there to add to the atmosphere but, realistically, I just don't know. . . ." She peeked again. "Do you think Greer's ready yet?"

Jeff glanced at his watch, double-checked it against the grandfather clock that had hugged the north wall of the vestibule for more than a century. They were in sync. And Greer was due.

As if on cue (which was how the butler worked), Greer walked toward them, carrying a plastic container filled with popcorn balls. "That's the last of them." He stacked it atop two others next to a plastic jack-o'-lantern full of candies positioned at the foot of the stairs. "We are ready for our guests."

As he did every year, Greer would keep the old basket on the porch filled with the treats as Jeff doled out popcorn balls to the steady stream of regulars who would begin showing up at dusk.

Sheila flipped switches. Amber light streamed through the windows and down the stairs toward the front walk. Notes from a dirge (Jeff presumed it was the same CD that had been used for his birthday party) drifted from the porch by way of outside speakers that Greer had set up that afternoon. Poe tried to sing along but it came out as "Frosty the Snowman."

Jeff said, "It's Halloween, and Edgar Allan Poe is singing a Christmas song?"

Sheila grinned sheepishly as she stepped away from the

door. "I tried to teach him something spooky but"—she shrugged, and turned her gloved palms toward the ceiling—"I finally gave up."

"This should be entertaining." Jeff nodded to Greer, who opened the double doors wide. A golden glow from all the lights washed over the oak floor.

Jeff stepped onto the porch as the walkway crowded with chattering, costumed children. Greer lifted the antique basket filled with the gaily wrapped popcorn balls and followed his employer out the door.

⎯⎯⎯

The witch was missing three teeth.

"Trick or treat?" she said softly.

Shy, Jeff thought as he studied the little girl, dressed all in black with a witch's hat nearly as tall as she was.

"Treat, for being the prettiest witch in Seattle." She looked familiar, something about her large, sad eyes. But he realized that it was the shyness giving her the wide-eyed, anticipatory gaze.

They had gone through the popcorn balls in less than two hours, and then the jack-o'-lantern had been emptied. Jeff now dispersed individually wrapped candies from a large, stainless-steel mixing bowl from Sheila's stash.

Upon seeing the bowl, Poe had begun singing "Silver Bells," only his clipped tongue made it come out as "Silver Bowls." Jeff barked, "Poe!" in his own clipped manner, and the bird piped down. A few of the kids laughed but Jeff had noticed that many were leery of the squawking bird, and he made a mental note to recommend skipping this new tradition next year.

It was a banner year for little ghosts and goblins, and kids dressed as their favorite superheroes and hip-hop stars. Jeff reached into the large stainless-steel bowl and withdrew a large clump of individually wrapped bubble gum, jawbreakers, and miniature candy bars. While he did this, he wondered again about the missing teeth and whether the girl's parents considered the effect that the sugar would have on the remaining molars and bicuspids. (Her father, two stair steps below his daughter, was dressed like Darth Vader, right down to the mask and boots, and sporting a lightsaber that looked more like a mop handle in a nylon sheath.)

"Go on," Darth Vader growled as he nudged the girl-witch.

Jeff's chest tightened. *Impatience will be the downfall of America.*

The witch advanced to the next step.

He reached toward the witch's bag, holding the fistful of sweets in one hand and cradling the bowl against his torso with the other, when two things happened simultaneously: Poe, released from his cage by a kid who'd sneaked up and swung open the door, flew screeching and flailing toward Jeff as Darth Vader scooped up the girl-witch with his left arm and pointed the lightsaber he held in his right hand at Jeff's chest.

Instinctively, Jeff lifted the bowl as he twisted to avoid the panicked crow. Too late he saw a flash, followed by a puff of smoke, then a spurt of flames licked the tip of the cheap nylon sheath. *Not a lightsaber; not a saber at all. A gun.* The bullet cut through the stainless-steel with a resonating *ping* and struck him in the chest.

The large bowl flipped into the air and showered the steps with bright candies as the villain and his little witch fled.

Jeff struggled against the catapulting force, watched the stainless-steel bowl strike the porch boards—*gong*—then clang and warp its way toward the pair of superheroes. Startled, they ran screaming down the steep stairs, following a string of frightened children that put Jeff in mind of ribbons on a kite's tail. The kite disappeared as he dropped backward, creating the illusion that it had fallen from the sky.

He landed deadweight across the threshold. He tried to

blink, but his eyelids wouldn't respond. He first saw Greer's face, then the face of his wife, Sheila. *An angel.* He started to speak, but he couldn't breathe, he couldn't breathe. . . .

TWENTY-NINE

~~~

*J*EFF AWOKE WITH the sensation that an anvil had been dropped on his chest. This feeling was immediately followed by two sets of sharp little pains, one shooting through his left shoulder and the other down his left side. A million miles away, he heard voices against a background of steady beeps. He hoped the beeps meant his heart was still pumping.

He pivoted his head to the left a couple of inches. His wife sat next to the bed, staring at something red and white in her grip. "Sheila?" The sound of his weak, raspy voice surprised him, made him wonder if anyone could hear him.

"Oh, thank God." Her voice quivered. When she stood and faced him, he recognized the blood-stained cloth as his shirt. "Jeff, honey, I'm right here."

"Where?"

"He can't see me. Oh, God."

". . . see you. *Where?*"

"Oh, thank God. The hospital, Jeff."

"You were worried about getting lipstick on that shirt."

She laughed but she was crying, too; made it sound choked. "Do you remember what happened?"

He thought a moment. It was all there, till he blacked out shortly after falling. He tried to move, winced, settled back down. "How long ago?"

"Five hours, sir." Greer stepped into Jeff's field of vision.

". . . side hurts."

"Your lung collapsed, sweetheart. The doctor had to make a couple of incisions in order to reinflate it."

"Gun?"

"Gunshot, left shoulder. Clean, the doctor said."

"Police?"

"There's a guard at your door. Fleming saw to that first thing."

"Fleming? Is he here?"

"He was," Sheila said. "Then he left to look for the shooter. We need to let him know you're conscious. Greer stayed at the house and gave Chris a full report before joining us here."

"How did *you* get here?"

Sheila blinked. "I . . . I must've been in the ambulance with you. I guess." She surveyed the room, then stared wide-eyed at Jeff.

"Honey, focus on me," he said. "Make this space yours. Greer, bring whatever she needs."

"Yes, sir."

"Call Doctor Jenn, Diane Fleming, whatever you need to do."

"Okay." Sheila took a deep breath, and released it. "I hope that little girl is all right. Do you remember her?"

"The witch." Jeff couldn't fathom someone using a child like that.

Greer said, "It could be the only thread that might help the police find them."

Man. Child. Something about the scenario waited at the fringes of Jeff's memory, as if cloaked in offstage darkness. He couldn't see it. He reached up to touch his head.

"Be careful, hon," Sheila said. "Your head is nested in an inflated inner tube, because of your concussion."

With his right hand, he gingerly felt the back of his skull. It was like pressing fingerprints into foam rubber. *Man. Girl. Father, daughter.* Jeff remembered the father and daughter who talked to Blanche about majolica. He remembered her phone calls to the police. "Blanche?"

"She and Trudy are out in the waiting room," Sheila said. "They went down there about twenty minutes ago to have some hot tea."

A curtain lifted. "Blanche. Get her."

"But—"

". . . important." He looked at Greer, who nodded and left the room.

"Bullet?"

Sheila said, "Forty-four."

"And I'm still alive?" He breathed as if he'd just run a mile.

"It went through the stainless-steel mixing bowl, which the doctor said deflected it enough to save your life. Poe helped. It was a chain of events, really. The child who opened Poe's cage, your turning toward Poe who was flying toward you. Chris said that when you're better, he'll tease you about your life being saved by a crow named Poe. Seriously, though, if the bullet hadn't deflected as it passed through the bowl, it would've . . ." Her voice trailed off for a moment before she said, "The doctor warned that for the rest of your life you'll feel it when it's going to rain."

"We live in Seattle."

"That's what I said. He just shrugged and said he'd check back in when you regained consciousness."

"Before we let him know that I have, I want to talk to Blanche. Fleming, too."

Blanche entered the room, took one look at Jeff, and covered her mouth with her hand. When she found her voice, she said, "They said you were going to be okay, but I'm glad to see it for myself."

Jeff smiled weakly. "Blanche, you remember telling me about the girl who was doing a school report on majolica?"

"Of course. Why?"

"Greer," Jeff said, "get Fleming back here."

Greer nodded, hurried to the door and spoke to the officer on guard duty.

Jeff looked at Blanche. "I need you to tell the detective about them."

Blanche looked from Jeff to Sheila and back again. "I . . . did that, Jeffrey, don't you remember? On Monday?"

"Of course I remember. I mean, go over it again, okay?"

"Of course."

"I'd bet my life it's the same pair from tonight."

"You almost did," Blanche said.

"Yeah, but why was he after me, and not Lanny? I didn't think anyone was in danger, since Lanny was put back in jail."

Blanche said, "Maybe the detective will find the man, and be able to get some sort of answer out of him. And, of course, help that poor girl."

After a moment, Greer returned. "The guard said Detective Fleming was called to a hotel near the airport. It's believed the suspect is checking out with the child, presumably for a flight."

"Does he think no one's going to look for them?"

"I don't know, sir. Something was said about multiple IDs." Greer returned to his self-appointed post as sentinel of his employer's side of the door.

Blanche said, "The detective knows all of us are here. He'll be back as soon as he can. In the meantime, you need to rest." She kissed his cheek, then squeezed Sheila's hand. "You, too." Blanche left, and the room grew quiet. Soon, the entire hospital seemed to settle in for the night. A softly toned intercom voice announced that visiting hours were over. Shortly after that, the harsh light of the corridor's fixtures dimmed, and the soft-soled nurses seemed to go into stealth mode.

Jeff drifted off to sleep.

⸙

A glare from the hallway woke Jeff, and as if each tick of the clock dropped another photographic slide into the viewfinder of his mind, he pieced together a picture: *tick,* pain; *tick,* gun; *tick,* siren; *tick,* intruder. His eyes popped open. The man stepped forward, side-lit by a sliver of light from the jarred bathroom door.

"Fleming?" Jeff said hoarsely. "What time is it?"

"Almost four," said the detective. "Didn't mean to startle you."

Sheila stirred on the cot beside Jeff's bed. He supposed she'd sent Greer back to the house.

"It's okay, hon. Fleming's here."

"Chris," she said, "did you find the guy?"

"We found the guy."

"Thank you," she said fervently before rolling over and drifting back to sleep.

Fleming quietly moved a chair nearer to the bed and seated himself on it. "I sent your security home when I got here."

"You're that sure you got the right guy?"

"I'm that sure."

"So," Jeff said as he pressed the button to elevate the top half of the bed, "the SeaTac Hotel lead panned out. He was the shooter."

"Nope, wasn't him. But—are you ready for this?—he knew who we were after."

"Come on. Nothing's that coincidental."

"Exactly."

"Okay, so who is he? The one at the hotel?"

"He is the widower of John Smith's ex-wife."

Jeff sat forward. *Mistake.* Hot-poker pain splintered off from the shoulder wound and toward his left arm, his neck, his heart, and a hundred other points. He sucked in air and his face bunched up as he grabbed for the shoulder with his good hand. He exhaled in a gust, and the sensation bottomed out with a thud in his groin. Nausea soon followed.

"Sorry, Talbot, but you'd better brace yourself if you want the whole story. It's a good one."

Jeff swallowed, panted for air. A nurse came through the door, checked gauges, monitors, tubing, and, finally, Jeff. "Your monitors showed some stress, Mr. Talbot. Do you need something for pain?"

He probably did but he wasn't about to risk falling asleep before getting his bedtime story. "Check back in half an hour."

"Okay," she said doubtfully, then left the room without closing the door.

Jeff took a cleansing breath. "Go on."

"My assistant gathered up three units with two cops each, and high-tailed it to the Marriott. They scared the man and the girl half to death. Fortunately, there weren't any hotheads among the officers, and they got it sorted out rather quickly—thanks to documentation the guy had with him. He's not our killer. Turns out, there was some confusion as to what our source had first reported. This man was checking into the hotel, instead of checking out."

Jeff said, "I see this is going to get complicated. It would help if you gave me Lanny's ex-wife's widower's name. Have I got that right?"

"You have. His name is Mike Sanders."

"Smith, Sanders. Okay, go on."

"At the same time that our units were sorting this out with Sanders at the hotel, the real killer and his daughter, Allison—the one who's on our tapes and was at Mrs.

Appleby's tearoom—were meeting Allison's mother at SeaTac. He'd called his ex with some story about an urgent job, told her he needed her to come out here and get their daughter."

"Out here from where?"

"Cleveland. So, according to what they had arranged, the killer's ex-wife waited at the airport after arriving with Mike Sanders and his girl."

"Are you telling me there are two guys with half-grown daughters?"

"That's right."

"What's their connection? And, don't tell me the shooter hired Sanders to help throw off the cops, like in *The Thomas Crown Affair*." Jeff pictured the museum scene where Brosnan's character brought in several identically dressed men in order to create a diversion.

"Nope." Fleming sighed. "You watch too many movies."

"That's because they're supposed to make sense when real life doesn't."

"Point taken." Fleming repositioned himself on the chair. "The girls are in dance class together in Cleveland. Every week, while the students study ballet and tap, the parents who hang around stay in a waiting room—mostly mothers but a few dads, too. One of the mothers was your buddy Lanny's ex-wife."

"The lady who owned the majolica statue."

Fleming nodded once. "Yeah. She found out last December she had breast cancer. Some Christmas present, huh? Anyway, Mike Sanders's statement backs up what Lanny told us. Janet Sanders and Lanny Smith were forced into an annulment by his parents. It crushed them both, so much so that Lanny broke off all connection with his family and left the East Coast. Janet went back home to live with her folks. A year or so later she moved to Cleveland to start a new life."

"And that's where she met Mike Sanders?"

"Right. Let me get back to our killer and the connection, first." Fleming cleared his throat. "Janet Sanders learned throughout the weeks in the dance studio waiting room that one of the fathers was a private investigator. When she knew she was dying, she hired him to try to find John Smith—Lanny. Her husband—"

"Mike Sanders."

"Right, Mike Sanders. He didn't know she'd done this. He found out while going through her things after her death—processing stuff, getting things in order. Now, here's where it gets crazy."

"Like it isn't already?"

Fleming grinned tightly, then got back to his story. "Sanders tried to contact the private eye, and the police show up on his doorstep."

"Wait. Whose doorstep?"

"Mike Sanders. The police had cross-referenced information because the PI—whose name is Greg Robertson, by the way—hadn't returned his daughter to her mother Thursday night. Because they shared custody and home-schooling duties, he'd taken the girl for his allotted vacation time during October, instead of during the summer."

It was coming together. Jeff said, "So, he's been in the Seattle area for three weeks?"

"Exactly. Air and hotel records—which were challenging, because he had multiple IDs—show that he arrived two days before Fiona Brock was killed." Fleming sat back, clearly satisfied.

"Wait," Jeff said. "He's a private eye, and he killed Fiona and Mustang Sally?"

"And, don't forget, tried to kill you. It's safe to assume he saw you with Sally."

"But this guy was a licensed PI!"

"And, this is the real world," Fleming added. "They can't all be like Philip Marlowe."

"What did he hope to gain by doing all this?"

"The root of all evil: money."

"So, the PI gig was a front?"

"No, I'm sorry to say. He's a bona fide PI—until Ohio learns about all this and revokes his license. He's crossed the line a few times, ended up in hot water out there. He had lied to Fiona Brock. Well, I shouldn't say lied. He apparently told her he had some information for Lanny that would make him a very happy man, but that he had to be sure Lanny was the man he was searching for. That's where the majolica piece came in."

"You mean it was used to verify Lanny's identity?"

"Right. The majolica piece confirmed it was Smith, because it had one-of-a-kind markings."

"The *J*s," Jeff said. "For John and Janet."

"You got it. Fiona agreed to help Robertson set up the test, to see if Lanny took the bait. He did, of course, and nearly went crazy when he saw the photos of the majolica.

"But the original plan, which was to find Lanny," Fleming continued, "wasn't going to net the PI any money now that Janet Sanders was dead, so he came up with a new plan: pressure her widower into paying him to keep quiet about Lanny."

Jeff had been keeping everything straight. Now, he lost ground fast. "Wait. Surely this Sanders guy knew that his wife had been married before."

"Oh, he knew all right. You're forgetting one key element."

"Well, Detective, you'll forgive me if I'm off my game. I've been under a little stress lately."

Fleming smiled. "Think it through, Talbot. It'll be good exercise for your brain."

"Okay." Jeff considered everything that had been thrown into the soup. "We've got *who* but, as I've said all along, it's the *why*, isn't it? At first, I thought it was 'Why does Lanny want the majolica?'"

Fleming said, "That was to get the provenance in order to try to find his ex-wife. He believed she would stick to her promise never to dispose of it. When he saw it on the market, he knew something had happened to her. He wanted to learn what that was."

Jeff noticed that he'd slid toward the footrail. He gingerly pushed himself back to the head of the bed. "Okay. The next *why* was 'Why did Fiona sell it out from under him?' We learned when we found it in the closet that she hadn't sold it at all. Now, we know it was . . . what? To trap Lanny?"

"The majolica was simply used to confirm that Lanny was Janet Sanders's ex-husband."

"Right, right." Jeff thought for a second. "I think there's only one question left, then, and it's also a *why* question: Why did Janet Sanders want to find Lanny before she died? I mean, she's had, like, a decade to try to locate him. Typically, I'd say it was because she was dying. I mean, I could buy that scenario if she'd never remarried. But she and this Mike Sanders have a daughter together."

"And, there's the rub," Fleming said triumphantly. "If you had exact dates, you'd have to figure your math a little differently. Sanders isn't the girl's biological father. Lanny is."

THIRTY

"Lanny?" **JEFF GRIPPED** the sheets with his good hand, fought the urge to spring from the bed.

"According to the stepfather. The girl, too, for that matter. Her mother had told her the whole thing before she died."

"Has anyone told Lanny?"

"Yeah. I was with him for an hour before I came over here."

"How's he taking it?"

"Like he's been hit with a stun gun."

"I would imagine." Jeff repositioned the protective doughnut behind his skull. "He's out of jail, right?"

"Of course. Apparently, he stopped by here as soon as I released him; guard told me. You were out like Aunt Tillie's teeth."

"I wish he had woke me up. I . . . he's got a lot to deal with, and I'd like to help him if I can."

"A preliminary meeting is being arranged to address the paternity issue. Smith hopes you'll be able to attend."

"I'll be there, one way or another." Jeff was quiet for a minute. "What about the weapon in Lanny's truck?"

"As a PI, Robertson had tracked down Smith. Therefore, he knew Smith's vehicle. We assume he let the air out of one of the tires in hopes that Smith would leave it for the time being."

"Which he did."

Fleming nodded. "After Robertson killed Fiona Brock to keep her quiet about her part in the affair, he went out the back door and tossed the weapon into the camper shell. When the weapon didn't show up, though, and you convinced the judge that Smith wasn't a flight risk, the killer's plans were hindered. He stayed in town to do what he could to strengthen the case against Lanny."

Jeff said, "Tell me again: Why did he need a case against Lanny?"

Fleming sighed wearily. "Robertson's client died. That was Lanny's ex-wife. He then decided to find Lanny, frame him for murder to keep him from claiming custody of his daughter. Then he was going to extort money from Sanders—the stepfather—or go to the authorities and claim the murder was Sanders's idea to begin with."

The detective glanced at his watch. "Sun'll be up soon. I'd better let you get some sleep."

"Thanks, Detective. For everything."

"To protect and serve. You remember."

Jeff swallowed. "I do remember."

⟅⟆⟅⟆

"Happy November, Mr. Talbot."

Jeff awoke to find a doctor and a nurse standing at his bedside on the right. Sheila rubbed his left hand. The nurse jotted notes on a clipboard.

November. He hoped the calendar was on One, and that it hadn't been days since Fleming had told him everything. All this sedation had him screwed up. "I expect it to turn out better than October did. Can I go home today?"

The doctor smiled. "I don't see why not. Nurse Turner will be back after rounds to instruct you on what you can and can't do." The nurse flashed a smile at Jeff that was clearly meant to elicit trust. The doctor added, "Just have someone call my office tomorrow, set up an appointment for you to come in on Friday to have that shoulder looked at."

They left, and Jeff and Sheila watched a movie on the small TV, had lunch, and napped before they saw Nurse Turner again.

She instructed Jeff on how to use the breathing apparatus for strengthening his reinflated lungs. Prescription slips, instruction sheets, and a page of telephone numbers were handed to Sheila, along with quick explanations.

"So, I'm free to go?" Jeff said.

"Almost." The nurse flashed another one of those chipper smiles. "We're waiting on the lab results of your last blood work-up. Precautionary measure. As soon as they're in, I'll let you know."

After she left, Jeff fiddled with the breathing machine, flipped through a magazine, sat on the edge of the bed, felt woozy, stretched back out, surfed TV channels, and sighed impatiently.

Sheila said, "Are you sure you're up to going home?"

"Sheila, I don't care if they have to wheel me to the car on a stretcher, I'm sleeping in my own bed tonight."

"Oka-ay," she said, stretching the syllables with sing-song doubt.

He watched her, amazed that she wasn't displaying any panic over her surroundings. "You're handling all this pretty well."

"Better than I expected I would. Dr. Jenn's been here a

couple of times while you were napping, and she said she'll ride home with us if I need her to."

"That's good of her."

"That's how she is. I mean, it'll cost us, but I know that her care and concern are genuine."

"Do you think we'll be home for dinner?"

"Don't tell me you aren't enjoying the hospital food."

"I'm spoiled. My wife's a pretty good cook."

"Thank you." Sheila straightened the stack of magazines on the wheeled tray. "It might be easier if it's dark when I leave here. Feels more confined, you know?"

"In that case, I'll try to be a patient patient."

Jeff opened a notepad on the tray, and was jotting FBI anagrams when Fleming showed up. "Hey!" Jeff said when the detective entered the room.

Fleming laughed. "You're awfully cheerful for someone who got shot last night."

Sheila smiled. "He's *patiently* waiting to be released. I'm sure he's excited to see anyone who might help him pass the time."

Fleming pulled up a chair. "I'll contribute a few minutes, if I'm not interrupting."

"Like Sheila said, we're just killing time." Jeff handed him the notepad.

"I'd forgotten that you do this when you're sorting out things." Fleming read aloud the column of phrases:

"Felon Being Investigated. Funny But Irritating. Fugitive Brigand Iced. Fatal Bowl Incident." He looked at Jeff. "Fatal bowl incident?"

"Yeah, I heard that the bowl didn't make it. I suppose I'll have to replace it, or my resident chef will go on strike."

"That's right," Sheila said, changing the channel to another movie.

"What happened here?" Fleming tapped the last one. It read: Frightening Blast I.

Jeff glanced at the pad, raised his good shoulder a fraction of an inch. "They don't all work out."

"Tell me about it."

"What are you doing here, anyway? You miss me?"

"Yeah, right. Actually, I brought Mom by. She wanted to see if she could be of any help."

"Where is she?" Sheila asked.

"Right here," Diane said as she entered the room behind a large bouquet of flowers. "I stopped by the gift shop."

Sheila embraced her friend, oohed and aahed over the flowers, and was obviously relieved to have reinforcement.

Nurse Turner entered with a wheelchair.

Jeff stood. "I don't have to ride in that, do I?"

"Hospital rules," she said in a tone that revealed she'd said it more times than she cared to remember, and enough times that she knew how to enforce it.

Dr. Jenn squeezed in past the nurse, and, while Sheila introduced her to Diane, Nurse Turner said, "I suppose we'll have to let you go home. Anyone else drops by, we'll have to get a larger room."

"In that case . . ." Jeff situated himself in the chair, and the nurse wheeled him to the exit with his entourage in tow.

Greer had parked the Jimmy just outside the sliding glass doors. Jeff stood, looped his good arm around Sheila, held her tight. "Sheila?"

"Uh-huh?" Her voice quavered a bit.

"I'm not much to look at, and I realize I'm now officially middle-aged. You sure you want to stick it out?"

"For better or worse, remember? In situations like this, though, you got stuck with 'worse.'"

"Not true. Now, just look into my eyes, click your heels together, and say, 'There's no place like home.'"

She laughed, and fixed her gaze on her husband's face as he walked her outside.

THIRTY-ONE

✤

*T*HE SUITE OF offices took up the entire nineteenth floor of a high-rise known locally (thanks to its domed sea-green cap) as the Ban Roll-On Building.

Jeff was winded by the time he and Lanny stepped from the box that had catapulted them lightning-quick to an eye-level view of the Space Needle.

It beat the alternative, though, and he reconsidered his judgment call about elevators only four days prior. He could barely manage a single flight of stairs in his own home, let alone several.

He steadied himself on a credenza under a large mirror that reflected floor-to-ceiling windows looking out on Puget Sound.

"You sure you're up to this?" Lanny asked.

Jeff reminded himself that it had been only three days since he'd been shot, and the doctor had told him it might

take weeks to fully regain his strength. "I'm fine. Use it or
lose it, right? Well, not much till I get rid of this sling but
you know what I mean."

"Thanks for coming with me." Lanny cleared his throat.
"I'm not sure how to handle this, or what to do, or what not
to do. I suppose I should request a DNA test but I'm not
sure whether that matters."

"It matters if you're unsure about being her father."

"You know that saying, 'Anyone can be a father, but it
takes someone special to be a daddy'? There could be
something to that."

"You're special, Lanny. Don't let anyone tell you different."

"Not to her, I'm not. In her eyes, I'm just a stranger who
might be threatening to take her from the only life she's
ever known. And, she's already lost her mother."

Jeff wasn't a father, so he couldn't say what core feelings Lanny might have when he first laid eyes on the girl
who was allegedly his own flesh and blood. "You'll know
what to do."

"God, I hope so."

Jeff glanced again at the young man beside him. The
makeover, although subtle, had made a big difference. It
had been courtesy of Greer and Sheila, and they'd understood that Lanny still wanted to be Lanny. The fingerless
gloves, tattered hat, and shabby clothes had been set aside
for new black corduroy trousers and a charcoal gray turtle-
neck under an open, black cord overshirt with a squared-
off tail. He still had a beard and long hair but they had been
expertly shaped, and the hair was clamped into a ponytail
at the nape of the neck. One might take him for an artist or
a poet.

A pleasant-looking woman pushing sixty for all it was
worth—and clearly proud of it—smiled as she circled
from behind a reception desk. She wore a navy suit with a
blouse printed all over with tiny pink and blue flowers, and
low-heeled shoes.

She could've been the model for what grandmothers used to look like—before pilates and South Beach had turned them into fifty-is-the-new-thirty knockouts.

"May I help you, gentlemen?" she said.

Jeff thought he smelled chocolate chip cookies, and wondered whether someone had brought in home-baked treats, or if plump grandmas with fluffed white hair and spectacles perched on button noses came eau de brown sugar.

Lanny said, "Yes, ma'am, we're here for the meeting with Detective Fleming."

"Yes, of course. Follow me." She led them along a large, circular corridor with glass-walled conference rooms forming its perimeter. The conference room was compliments of a top-notch Seattle attorney whom Chris Fleming had been dating for the past six months.

"Here we are." The woman indicated a large mahogany door surrounded by more glass. "Let me know if you need anything."

Lanny thanked her, then held the door for Jeff.

Inside, Chris Fleming sat at the head of a conference table the size of a barge, visiting with a man who looked like you'd expect a man to look after cancer had taken his wife and left him to raise a daughter alone. Jeff figured time would help erase the lines and lift the weight off tired shoulders.

The pair stood when Lanny and Jeff entered.

"Mike," Fleming said to the man, "I'd like you to meet John Landon Smith. Lanny, Mike Sanders."

Jeff observed as the two men shook hands. After initial reactions (Sanders's stunned expression at his first sight of Lanny, and Lanny looking as nervous as Dry Rot in a dog pound), both men seemed relieved to have step one behind them.

Fleming then introduced Jeff to Sanders, and after Jeff had shaken the man's hand, the four of them sat two and two across from one another at the table. Jeff guessed

Sanders was closer to his own age than to Lanny's. His hair was black but the temples showed plenty of gray. He had sad eyes.

"I'm sorry about your arm, Mr. Talbot," Sanders said.

"Don't be. And call me Jeff, by the way."

Fleming said, "I'm sure we'll all be more at ease if we drop the formalities."

The men nodded in agreement, then Jeff continued. "From what I understand, you were instrumental in connecting the dots."

"Most of the credit goes to Angela. That's Allison's mother."

"I hope I get a chance to thank her."

Fleming said, "You will. She's down the hall with the girls."

"Look, Lanny." Mike Sanders sighed heavily, and his shoulders seemed to drop even more. "Obviously, it was important to Janet that you know about Julia. Otherwise, she wouldn't have hired someone to find you. I won't lie to you: It was hard for me to accept, at first, that she wanted to tell you about your daughter."

"I can understand that."

"I loved Janet very much. It's been an extraordinary loss."

"I understand that, too," Lanny said. "I loved her, and lost her to something beyond my control. She was an amazing person."

Mike's eyes widened, and he smiled. "She was, wasn't she?"

The two men stared at each other for a moment.

"Tell you what," Mike said. "I'll tell you about her last ten years, if you'll tell me about the ten before that."

"I'd like that."

Fleming stood. "Why don't Jeff and I give you two a few moments alone. We'll check on the girls."

Jeff squeezed Lanny's shoulder, then followed Fleming

from the room. When they were out of earshot, he said, "I'd hate to be in their shoes."

"No joke." Fleming led the way down the corridor. "Even Solomon would have trouble with this one. It's easy to tell that both those men are caring people."

Fleming stopped in front of a door, and knocked. "Wait'll you see this."

A slender woman in her early thirties with light brown hair answered, and smiled slightly when she saw Fleming.

After the pair entered the room, Fleming said, "Jeff, this is Allison's mother, Angela Robertson. Angela, Jeff Talbot."

She clamped her hand to her mouth, and blinked back tears. "I'm so glad you're okay. I . . . I just wish . . ." She paused, shook her head.

Jeff said, "I'm fine. Really."

"Thank you. It's, well, I always fall apart after a crisis is over." She dabbed at her eyes with her fingertips.

Jeff suspected that things were far from over for the woman but he knew what she meant. He looked past her, to the far corner where Blanche Appleby entertained two girls. "I see you're in capable hands."

"She's a treasure, that one. Allison phoned me several days ago, right after she'd had tea with Blanche at her shop. She couldn't stop talking about her, and how nice everything was."

Blanche had obviously thought of everything. A small, round table was draped with vintage linens, and held a centerpiece of harvest mums in yellows and oranges. On a side table were all sorts of goodies for a proper English tea.

Angela said, "Blanche has been telling them the history of the tea set they're drinking from, and how Fergie never travels without her own tea set packed in a fitted case similar to the one there on the table. Those girls won't rest now till they have their own set."

"If I had to guess," Jeff said, "I'd say Blanche has already gotten them each one to take home."

They joined Blanche and the girls at the table. The girls turned toward them, and Jeff quickly masked his initial reaction.

If it were always this obvious, the courts wouldn't need DNA evidence to prove paternity. The resemblance was remarkable. The bone structure, the olive skin, and those eyes. This girl's eyes were exact duplicates of Lanny's. There was no arguing: Lanny was this child's father.

Now he understood Sanders's reaction when he'd first seen Lanny. And, he remembered what Lanny had said about being a daddy. This was going to be a challenge.

"Ladies, we have company," Blanche said. She introduced everyone. Jeff could see that Blanche's innate kindness and tact had helped both girls, who had just come through traumatic transitions in their young lives, to find a kind of normalcy. Allison, who had seen her father shoot Jeff, seemed to be looking everywhere but at the sling on his arm. He could only imagine what conflicting emotions were passing through her small body.

It may not have been as bad as all that, he realized upon reflection. Everything had happened so fast on Halloween night that she might have only been aware of confusion. But whatever counseling she might need in the future to deal with her father's crimes, Jeff knew the healing had begun right here.

After a few moments of small talk, the girls drifted away so Julia could show Allison a new dance step she'd missed at the previous week's lesson.

Jeff had been toying with a notion ever since Fleming's remark about Solomon. Finally, he said, "I have an idea . . ."

Females are a persuasive lot. Get a group of them to embrace an idea, and a man doesn't have a chance. By the time Jeff had shared his idea, all four females were excitedly making plans. There's nothing like something new and exciting to turn a child's mind from the troubled past to the bright future.

Fleming said, "Hold on, now. Like Jeff said, we'll need to check with Julia's dad, and see what he thinks about all of this."

Jeff wondered whether Fleming meant Mike Sanders or Lanny. Then, he realized it was a safe way to say both.

Jeff and Fleming escorted the girls, along with Blanche and Angela, to the room where they'd left Lanny and Mike. Through the glass wall, Jeff saw that the men seemed comfortable with each other, talking, smiling.

When they entered the room, Julia seated herself next to Mike Sanders, then looked across the table. "Wow, you look like Jesus. I'm Julia."

Lanny smiled. "I thought as much. You look like your mother."

Julia shrugged so fast it was more like a twitch. "She told me that I look like you. But *nobody* told me that you look like Jesus."

"I looked very different when I knew your mother."

"Uh-huh," she said. "I've got pictures."

"I'd like to see them sometime."

Her shoulder twitched again. "Sure."

Allison tilted her head and studied Lanny as if he were a painting. "You look like both of them, Jules."

Resilient, Jeff thought. These girls would be okay.

Fleming said, "Who wants to tell them the idea?"

"I do! I do!" the girls chimed in unison.

Despite both girls chattering and laughing and planning and pleading, combined with both women interjecting facts and offering assurances, Lanny and Mike got the gist of the solution: If they would agree, Angela would escort the girls to Seattle each summer, where they would stay with Blanche and have plenty of time to visit with Lanny.

Both Lanny and Mike seemed pleasantly surprised by the idea, and Jeff left it to the group to iron out details.

Greer waited out front beside the woodie. He saw Jeff, and got out to help his employer with the door. Jeff hoped he'd be independent soon, but the old car's lack of power steering was going to be a challenge.

When they arrived home, the spinster sisters' white van was backed up to the side of the house near the kitchen door.

"Sheila's really going through with it," Jeff said, a little surprised.

"Looks that way, sir." Greer guided the woodie around the van's nose and parked it.

Jeff approached the open rear doors of the van and peered inside. Bargain Basement, Morty, and Poe stared back from their perches in three transport cages.

"It's for your own good, you know," Jeff said.

No response.

"You'll be much happier with bird people, a place where you can rule the roost."

Nothing.

"Rule the roost, get it?"

Silence.

"Oh, *now* you stop talking. Well, anyway, thanks, Poe."

"Sayonara," Poe squawked.

Jeff passed Polly and Lucy on their way out. They greeted him happily, then closed up the van, climbed in, and drove off.

Jeff found Sheila sitting at the refectory table in the kitchen. "Are you sure you wanted to do that?" he asked her.

"I'm sure. I had to try it but I realized that the only reason I got them was because I found birdcages in the conservatory. Polly and Lucy have gone nuts over them every time they've been here. It's a good decision."

Greer brought in the mail, handed it to Sheila with a slight bow, then went into the butler's pantry.

She sorted through the stack and handed a bundle to

Jeff. Then she pulled two magazines from her own bundle and held them up for him to see.

Jeff glanced at the covers, and shook his head. Bird magazines.

She said, "Don't you think we can cancel these subscriptions?"

About the Author

Before moving to Michigan, Deborah Morgan was managing editor of a biweekly newspaper located on the fifteen miles of Kansas Route 66. As with most editors of small-town papers, Morgan wore the reporter's and photographer's hats, too. Morgan and her husband, author Loren D. Estleman, go antiquing every chance they get. For more information, visit her Web site at www.deborahmorgan.com.